Dear Reader,

Is there anything sexier than a man who knows how to fix your car? My husband once changed a dead battery in my car, and I was all over him! And it's not that we women can't do it ourselves, but really, who wants to?

Okay, some of us do. Just not me. Ever.

That's why my heroine, Hailey Fitzwilly, surprised me. She willingly agrees to work in a motorcycle garage. And yes, that means getting grease on her hands—and believe me I avoid all forms of grease! Sure she's motivated by making her domineering mother (again, not writing from experience) happy. Oh, and there's the little matter of the hottie who owns the garage. Kid Cassidy is a gorgeous man who knows his way around an engine...so you can guess Hailey's reaction to him! (Hint: see first paragraph.)

I hope you enjoy reading Hailey's rollicking adventures as much as I enjoyed writing them.

Keep on laughing,

Jennifer McKinlay

P.S. Online readers can praise me, uh, I mean write me at jenymck@hotmail.com.

He handed her a beer and asked, "Do you need a glass?"

She had been in advertising long enough to know that one always mimicked a client. It made them feel at ease and built rapport. He didn't have a glass, so she said, "No, thanks."

His glance was mocking. Obviously her mimicking tactic wasn't going to melt the ice. "You don't like me very much, do you?"

"It's not personal," he said. "It's not you so much as your type."

No way was she a type! But she couldn't resist asking, "Really? And what's that?"

"Well-bred, rich girl desperately seeking a doctor for a husband," he said.

Ouch! The crack hit a little too close to home, even if it was more her mother's idea than her own. "What makes you say that?"

"How many young, single women zip around in a Mercedes?"

"Hey! I earned that car."

"Doing what?" His voice was ripe with doubt.

He wanted to give her attitude? She'd show a little of her own. "High-priced hooker with a *very* exclusive clientele." Satisfaction was hers when he choked on his drink.

Keeping Up Appearances

Jennifer McKinlay

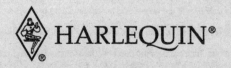

HARLEQUIN®

TORONTO • NEW YORK • LONDON
AMSTERDAM • PARIS • SYDNEY • HAMBURG
STOCKHOLM • ATHENS • TOKYO • MILAN • MADRID
PRAGUE • WARSAW • BUDAPEST • AUCKLAND

ISBN 0-373-44213-0

KEEPING UP APPEARANCES

Copyright © 2005 by Jennifer Orf.

This edition published by arrangement with Harlequin Books S.A.

® and TM are trademarks of the publisher. Trademarks indicated with ® are registered in the United States Patent and Trademark Office, the Canadian Trade Marks Office and in other countries.

www.eHarlequin.com

Printed in U.S.A.

ABOUT THE AUTHOR

Jennifer McKinlay spent most of her childhood talking to herself. In fact, her fantasy life was so rich with imaginary friends that she started writing it down to keep it all straight. Naturally, she became an author. Now all grown-up, her life is still full of imaginary friends but she has to make room for the imaginary friends of her sons as well. It makes for quite a full house, and at any given meal there might be a place setting for a train, a sea turtle or a butterfly. You just never know. Jennifer lives in Arizona with her musician husband Chris, their two sons, a dog, a cat and four fish.

Books by Jennifer McKinlay

HARLEQUIN DUETS
74—TO CATCH A LATTE
104—THICK AS THIEVES

Don't miss any of our special offers. Write to us at the following address for information on our newest releases.

Harlequin Reader Service
U.S.: 3010 Walden Ave., P.O. Box 1325, Buffalo, NY 14269
Canadian: P.O. Box 609, Fort Erie, Ont. L2A 5X3

For my fabulous editor Wanda Ottewell.
All I can say is—Thanks!

1

WITH HER BUTT PROPPED IN the air, Hailey Fitzwilly felt all of the blood rush to her head. The rhythmic strains of sitar music filled the room and Hailey concentrated on her breathing and her downward-facing-dog posture. She was filled with a sense of peace. It made the past six months of studying and training for her newly-framed yoga in-structor's certificate worth it, for this was what had drawn her to yoga—the silence and the stillness.

Gone was her hectic life as an advertising executive. No more rising at four-thirty in the morning to hop on the com-muter train bound for Manhattan. No more clients sucking the life out of her with their demented demands for celebrity pitchmen and eye-level product placement in every store in the country. And no more being introduced as the woman who revolutionized the way adult diapers were marketed. If someone sang the "Tinkle, Tinkle, I'm a Big Star" jingle to her one more time, she was afraid she'd injure them.

With blood filling her temples, Hailey could almost block out the memory of the day her career crashed and burned. Almost. Her knees wobbled. She focused on her breathing. She was okay. It had happened months ago and now it was all just a painful memory.

Upon reflection, she knew that it was the success of that campaign that had killed her career. She had managed to get the adult-diaper company to pony up the money to pay one of Hollywood's notorious stars of old to pitch the campaign. It hadn't been too difficult. Kyle Weatherby, B-movie actor and heartthrob of the fifties, had been in rehab and was about to be tossed out on his caboose because he was broke. Hailey had contacted his agent and—bang—the next thing she knew she had a well-liked celebrity pitchman who had actually turned the sweet children's rhyme into a charismatic little ditty about peeing your pants. It was a huge hit in advertising circles, and Hailey was a star.

Advertising is an ugly business, however, and not all of Hailey's colleagues were happy about her success. She endured a lot of jokes about incontinence and nappies, and it seemed someone always wanted to torture her by humming that damn jingle.

She began taking yoga classes with her current business partner, Madeline, in an effort to ease some of her stress. But she forgot to breathe, and when Denny Plewicky kept humming the jingle under his breath while she was trying to pitch the biggest campaign of her life to Nike, she became unglued.

She had been working a lot of overtime on the Nike deal. Being an ad exec was sort of like being a junkie. You were always jonesing for the next big campaign that would make your product a household word like Kleenex or Mr. Coffee. Hailey had been ready for her next big campaign, but the adult diapers wouldn't go away.

In the middle of her PowerPoint presentation to the bigwigs at Nike, Danny Plewicky had kept humming the jingle. It had ruined her concentration and her momentum and halfway through her presentation, she found herself shrieking, "Enough! I hate adult diapers. I hate that stupid campaign and I really hate that damn jingle. I hate it, hate it, hate it! Now shut up!"

Danny and the rest of the room had been engulfed in a sudden silence. The only audible sound had been Hailey's career giving a death rattle as it died there on the boardroom floor.

Hailey shook her head and forced herself to keep breathing. She needed to look at the bright side. She hadn't hopped on to a commuter train bound for Manhattan in more than six months. Now she was her own boss. She set her own hours, and the only clients she had to please were people like herself, people seeking an escape from the hustle and bustle of their days. Hailey answered to no one.

A chiming version of the theme to *The Flintstones* broke through her concentration, jarring her out of her meditative state. Her cell phone was lying on the floor beside her mat. Nuts. She tried to ignore it but "Yabba Dabba Do" was relentless. Still upside down, Hailey reached for the phone. The display read *Mother*.

Hailey fell out of her downward-dog position and scrambled across the floor, away from the sitar music and into her office.

"Hello, Mother," she said, trying not to sound out of breath.

"Hailey, what's wrong? You sound odd," Selma Fitzwilly said.

"Do I?" Hailey asked, holding the phone away while she gasped for breath. "I just got out of a meeting."

Madeline, Hailey's partner, wandered into the office and reclined onto the hammock they had strung across the back wall. She was eating pot stickers out of a carton, and the smell made Hailey's stomach rumble.

"I hope they're not working you too hard at that agency," her mother said. "Do you want me to have your father call your boss?"

"No!" Hailey shouted. "Er...uh...what I mean is, no,

thank you. I think having Dad call my boss might be considered unprofessional."

Madeline paused with a pot sticker halfway to her lips and rolled her eyes. Hailey took the opportunity to filch the pot sticker from between the chopsticks. When Madeline's eyes returned to their upright position, she scowled at her empty chopsticks and then at the bulge in Hailey's cheek. She poked her with a chopstick before she resumed eating.

"Hailey, are you listening to me?" Selma demanded.

"Uh-huh," Hailey said.

"Don't mumble, dear. It's not ladylike," Selma chided.

Hailey swallowed the pot sticker whole. "Yes, Mother."

"Now as I was saying, the committee for the Fairfield County Children's Hospital charity auction is meeting Saturday morning," her mother said. "I was thinking you could pick me up and we could go together."

"Oh, you know I'd love to, but I have a..." Hailey's mind went blank and she cast a panicked look at Madeline. Madeline rolled out of the hammock and stood beside her.

"A seminar on the importance of jingle writing, Miss Fitzwilly," Madeline said loudly enough for Hailey's mother to hear her.

"Who is that?" Selma asked.

"My secretary," Hailey said. "I couldn't function without her."

Madeline beamed at her.

"Well, you'll just have to cancel your seminar," her mother said. "The Children's Hospital needs you."

Hailey volunteered at the Children's Hospital. She knew what they needed. They needed people to show up and spend some time with the kids. Sure the money from the auction helped to keep the hospital running, but Hailey disliked working on the auction with all of the local richy-rich who loved throwing galas for themselves in the name of charity but who would never think to be there when a poor kid needed his head held as he threw up after a rough round of chemo. The hypocrisy of the black-tie charity auction made her feel as if she would throw up.

"I'll be sure to make a hefty donation," she offered.

"Well, I suppose the children will just have to be happy with that." Selma heaved a sigh steeped in disapproval. "I'm sure they'll understand that the future wife of a prominent pediatrician is just too busy to make time for them and would prefer to write a check rather than roll up her sleeves and help put on a function in their behalf."

"I volunteer there every week," Hailey reminded her mother.

"I know, dear," Selma said. Her voice was sharp with impatience. "But this is one of the biggest events of the year. It's important and not just for you. We've worked on the auction committee for the past five years together. How will it look if you don't volunteer? What will people say? I just don't think I could bear the gossip."

Hailey felt her stomach clench. Only her mother carried guilt instead of pepper spray. Heaven help the poor slob who tried to mug her. He'd be in therapy for twenty years to get over it.

"All right, Mother," she said. "I'll pick you up at ten."

"Excellent," Selma said approvingly. "And wear that darling melon-colored suit that I bought for you. You'll look as lovely as a sunrise."

"Yes, Mother," Hailey agreed. "Goodbye."

She flipped the phone shut with a frown.

"Hailey, it's been three months since we opened the studio," Madeline said. "When are you planning on telling your parents that you're no longer a cog in the capitalist machine that grinds down the free will in us all?"

Hailey smiled. Only Madeline could make an ad job sound so dramatic.

"Any day now," Hailey answered with a grim smile. "Probably right after I have a lobotomy and ten sessions of electroshock therapy."

"Don't you think they'll be proud of you for starting your own business?"

"Dad might be," Hailey said. "But I'm not so sure about my mother. An advertising executive for a daughter is fine, because I'd meet the right sort of man, but she could never wrap her brain around a yoga teacher."

"She still wants you to marry a nice doctor or lawyer or king of some small, independent nation?" Madeline asked.

"Yep, that'd work," Hailey agreed.

"I bet you haven't even told your mother that you and Burke split up, have you?"

"Well…I meant to. There just never seemed to be a good time to mention that his housekeeper had given me the 'let's be friends' and 'it's not you it's me' speech for him. Jerk."

"But that was last summer," Madeline said. "It's been almost a year."

"I'm hoping my mother will just forget about him."

"A young, eligible pediatrician from a well-to-do family?" Madeline asked. "Yeah, right. That's like expecting a shark to just swim past the blood in the water."

"That's not my biggest problem right now," Hailey said. "You know that orange suit that my mother gave me for my birthday?"

"The one that makes you look like a road-construction cone?"

"Yeah, that's the one." Hailey cringed. "She wants me to wear it to a luncheon tomorrow."

"Uh-oh," Madeline said. "Didn't you donate it to some less fortunate, fashion-impaired individual?"

"I have one hour before my next class," Hailey said. "I've got to go and see if I can find it."

"Or you could tell your mother the truth?" Madeline suggested. "About everything."

"Ha-ha." Hailey grabbed her bag from the shelf and jammed her feet into a pair of flip-flop sandals that sported big pink daisies. "You're so funny."

"Don't worry if you're late. I can cover for you," Madeline shouted after her. Hailey waved as she raced out of the building.

"YOU'RE LATE." SELMA FROWNED at Hailey.

Selma was five feet four inches and that was in high heels, the only shoes she ever wore. She was wearing some sort of fluffy, fuchsia silk dress that ruffled around her throat, wrists and ankles. Completing the look was a red leather clutch and strappy red sandals. Hailey winced at the combo. Selma believed that if a six-foot-two, rail-thin model wore an outfit in Milan then that was what she would wear, because haute couture was highly regarded— and Selma was all about being highly regarded.

Selma had met John Fitzwilly in the small Italian town where she'd been raised while he was touring Europe. At the young age of seventeen, she married John Fitzwilly, left her home and never looked back. Unfortunately, she wasn't the debutante the Fitzwillys had intended for their son and they never let her forget that she didn't belong.

Thirty-three years later, Selma was still trying to find her niche. She wore the latest fashions and joined all of the right clubs and boards and committees, but she never felt

accepted into the community she tried so hard to be a part
of. Hailey wished she could tell her mother to accept herself and then the others would, too, but this was not something she could talk to her mother about. It would
devastate her to know that Hailey was aware of her quest
to belong.

"I'm sorry," Hailey said and kissed her mother's cheek
as she opened the passenger door for her. "I was held up."

"I'll bet Caroline Matthews never leaves her mother
waiting at the curb."

"Mother, you were inside watching a rerun of *Dr. Phil*,"
Hailey said as she climbed into the driver's seat and
started the engine.

Caroline Matthews, a former classmate of Hailey's, was
everything that Selma longed for Hailey to be. She had
married old money right out of college, produced two perfect heirs to the family fortune, was on every charity committee and was treasurer of the Junior League. Hailey
would rather hang herself than live that life, but Selma believed it was the pinnacle of female achievement. Hailey
sighed. It was going to be a long lunch.

"Nevertheless, punctuality is important," her mother
said. "Especially if you're going to be a doctor's wife. You
must never keep Dr. Burke waiting or he might not propose." Selma always used the *doctor* moniker, as if Hailey
might forget that he had a medical degree.

"I don't think he's going to propose—" Hailey began,
but Selma cut her off. "Nonsense. Of course he will. You're
a terrific catch. Why, just look at all you've accomplished."

Selma broke into an off-key rendition of Hailey's infa-
mous jingle. Hailey felt her stomach roll over. The ulcers
which had begun to plague her since her days in advertising began to bubble. Only her mother could trigger such
a reaction in her now. More accurately, it was the dual life

she was forced to live for fear of disappointing her mother that caused her stomach to back up like a sewer. She had to be honest with her.

It was on the tip of her tongue to tell her mother the truth about her breakup with Burke and be done with it.

"I just can't wait for the day that you become Mrs. Dr. Burke," Selma gushed. "That'll be the happiest day of my life."

Hailey swallowed her words. They went down as easily as a fistful of rocks.

Why was she such a wimp? Because she hated to disappoint her mother. And this would be more than a little disappointment. This was huge. This was the Titanic of disappointment.

Mercifully, the country club came into view. All Hailey had to do was be the dutiful daughter for an hour and a half. Surely she could do that.

"EAT YOUR FINGER SANDWICH, dear," Selma Fitzwilly chided her daughter. "You're looking a bit pale. Are you having a bout of bad stomach today?"

Everyone at the luncheon table turned to look at Hailey. She gave a small, tight-lipped smile and crouched lower in her seat. Oh, man, her life had just become an embarrassing television commercial.

"I'm fine," she whispered to her mother.

"Are you sure?" her mother persisted. "I have some Pepto in my purse."

Hailey heard someone at the table trying to cough over their laughter.

"Really, Mother, I'm fine," she said.

"All right, dear, but you just let me know if you need it." Her mother patted her hand and announced to the table in a stage whisper, "Hailey has a delicate constitution."

"Like IBS? My Morty had that irritable bowel syndrome until the day he died," Jean Parker said. She nodded her dyed red hair and took a healthy swig from her martini. She narrowed her gaze at Hailey and continued, "He was either on the pot for hours or not for days. Plum wore himself out."

Hailey forced her lips to curve up. She wanted to shriek, "No, not IBS," but Jean was her mother's closest friend. She was an outsider like Selma, and they had bonded years ago and never broke ranks. Jean was from the South and had worked to lose her twang just as Selma had worked to lose her Italian accent. But where Selma still worked to keep up appearances, Jean didn't really care anymore. Hailey was sure it had been at least fifteen years since she'd seen her without a drink in her hand.

The older ladies at the table nodded in agreement with Jean—IBS must be running rampant through the older folks—while the younger ladies at the table tried not to laugh too loudly.

Hailey sighed and stared down at her china plate, unable to meet the amused gazes of the ten ladies sharing their table. She supposed she should be glad her mother was obsessed with stomach ailments and not feminine hygiene. But now that she'd left advertising, she wouldn't even have bad stomach if her mother didn't make her such a guilt-ridden nervous wreck.

She wanted to pull the white tablecloth over her head. She refrained, opting to take a bite of the nasty, moon-shaped watercress sandwich her mother had selected for her. She hated watercress. Hailey wouldn't feed this sandwich to a dog.

She lifted the napkin from her lap and under the pretense of dabbing her mouth, she spit the sandwich into the napkin. When she lifted her head, she saw Caroline Matthews watching her with an amused half smile. Busted! Hailey quickly glanced away.

"Well, ladies, are we ready to discuss ideas for this year's Children's Hospital auction?" Caroline asked.

Hailey was relieved to have everyone's attention turned away from her bowels.

"I think we should empty our husband's wallets on something they will really enjoy bidding on," one of the ladies said.

"I agree," said Caroline with a grin. "We have a wonderful selection of donated items from the usual shops and we're charging two hundred and fifty per plate for attendees. But we need something truly fabulous for the silent auction. Something that will get the men into an out-and-out bidding war," she said. "Any ideas?"

"An all-expense-paid vacation for two?" suggested one committee member.

"You want that for yourself, Audry," Caroline teased, and the woman laughed in return.

Audry Wilcox was another former classmate of Hailey's. Blonde and bubbly, she was Caroline's best friend and she, too, strolled through life with an air of never having suffered so much as a bad hair day. This mystified Hailey. It was just a little too Stepford-wifey for her.

"Season tickets to the opera?" said another.

"No, no, no." Caroline shook her head. "Think like a man. What would get them to open their wallets?"

"Golf clubs," offered one of the older ladies.

"Good, but bigger," Caroline said. "It has to be something that they absolutely have to have, something that would get their testosterone boiling."

The women were all silent, staring one at another as if collectively willing an idea to come to them.

Hailey had an idea. She opened her mouth. She closed her mouth. She had a fabulous idea, but she knew her mother would object.

"Hailey?" Caroline said. "You look as if you were about to say something. Did you have an idea?"

Hailey shook her head. "No."

"Oh, come on," Caroline cajoled. "You're in advertising. You have your finger on the pulse of the people. What was that famous jingle you wrote? Your mother sings it all the time. It goes—"

"A chopper!" Hailey shouted. "How about a custom-built chopper?"

Several of the older ladies stared blankly at her.

"It's a motorcycle," she said. Selma would have a coronary, but Hailey would have done anything to save herself from having to hear the jingle again.

"No, they're too dangerous—" Selma began, but Caroline interrupted her. "Hailey, you're a genius!"

The other women at the table began to smile and nod. Hailey felt that spurt of adrenaline she used to get when a client loved her idea. She tried to take a few deep breaths to make it go away.

"Every man dreams of having a motorcycle," Caroline said. "My husband talks about buying one all of the time. It's very trendy nowadays, especially if it's custom made."

"There's a place in Fairfield where they design custom bikes. My brother bought one from them a few years ago," Hailey said. "We could ask them if they'd donate a motorcycle for the auction."

"Fabulous," Caroline said. "You're in charge of getting the motorcycle."

"Me?" Hailey blinked. Oh, this was perfect. It would take no time at all to solicit a donation and then she could go back to her real life.

"Hailey always does the invitations for the auction. She has such lovely design ideas," her mother said. "Don't you, dear?"

"I'm sure someone else could do just as well," Hailey said.

"Nonsense. You are gifted. You've won awards for your work," Selma Fitzwilly declared. "You'll just have to find someone else to get the motorcycle."

Hailey bit her cheek to keep from screaming. She wondered if there was a statute of limitations on being mortified by your mother. In her case, she felt as if she were serving a life sentence.

"Well, this year Hailey is going to be entirely too busy getting the motorcycle," Audry declared. "I can take over the invitations."

"Perfect," Caroline agreed.

Hailey unclenched her cheek in surprise. This was the first year that Caroline was sitting in her mother's place as chairwoman for the committee and it looked as if she was more than happy to flex her authority muscle. Well, right on. This lunch was looking up.

"There," Audry said. "It's all settled."

"Can you believe that woman?" Selma fumed at her daughter as they drove home from the luncheon. "She thinks she's so special just because her family can be traced back to the Mayflower. Well, I think she is just rude."

"Audry was just trying to help coordinate the auction, Mother," Hailey said as she gripped the Mercedes's steering wheel tighter than necessary.

"Well, did she have to take you off of the invitations? You always do such a lovely job." Selma pouted.

Hailey thought of the hundreds of paper cuts she had suffered over the years. Frankly, if she never licked another stamp in this lifetime she would die a happy woman.

"I'm sure Audry will do just fine," Hailey said, trying to soothe her mother's temper.

"Humph," Selma sniffed. "Just wait until I talk to Audry's mother about this. I'll get you back on invitations. Don't you worry."

The ilk feeling in Hailey's stomach intensified, reminding her of the time her mother had taken it upon herself to get Hailey a date for her middle school dance. Hailey had been asked by Simon Wentworth, but he hadn't met her mother's standards since he was one of the kids bussed in from the other side of town. Selma had been appalled at the thought of Hailey being seen with him. She had called the parents of every boy—well, every boy she deemed acceptable—in Hailey's class. They had all said no except for dork extraordinaire Chester Stevens.

Hailey had prayed for a broken arm, a case of the plague or even a tornado to flatten her school—anything to get out of the dance. Instead, she'd been forced to go to the dance with Chester. It had been the worst night of her thirteen-year-old life, compounded by the fact that to get even with her for rejecting him, Simon had told everyone that Hailey put out. Chester had believed him and called his mother to come and get him.

Hailey had spent the rest of the dance locked in a stall in the girls' bathroom. She had refused to leave it, even when the janitor had threatened to take the hinges off. It took months for the teasing to stop, and that only happened because Sandy Moreau's shorts fell down during the fifty-yard dash in gym class, thus replacing Hailey as the humiliation queen. To this day, Hailey still felt as though she owed Sandy one.

Hailey turned onto her parent's winding drive, hoping she didn't get sick before they parked.

"Mother, please don't say anything. I'm actually looking forward to a year off from designing the invitations. It's a lot of work and I've been very tired lately."

"Oh?" Selma said with a frown. "Let me feel your forehead. Do you have a fever? Why didn't you say anything sooner? I'll call Dr. Harris straightaway."

"Mother, no," Hailey said, feeling another cramp start. "I just need some rest and I'll be fine. Really."

"Nonsense," Selma said as she stepped out of the car and led the way up the steps and into the house. "I will worry myself silly if we don't call the doctor. You wouldn't want that, would you?"

Hailey had never seen her mother be silly about anything. She couldn't even imagine it. She practiced her *pranayama* breathing as she followed her mother into the house. Someday she was going to get a spinal implant and then she would be able to stand up to her mother. Someday.

AFTER A SHORT CONSULTATION over the phone with the ever-patient Dr. Harris, Hailey escaped her mother's house at a run. She was sure if anyone were watching they'd think she was an escapee from the ha-ha house. She sure felt like one.

Her long brown hair was twisted into a tight French knot and she still wore the designer suit her mother had requested. The orange color did nothing for her complexion, but she hadn't wanted to hurt her mother's feelings by changing before she left.

She glanced at her reflection in the rearview mirror as she drove down the driveway and was startled by the A-type professional woman looking back at her. It was hard to believe that she'd been wearing this outfit for three hours and it hadn't taken over her personality yet. It must be the orange color. It probably kept her from taking herself too seriously.

It hadn't been that long ago that she had been a type-A woman. Every day had been full of meetings and deadlines and overtime. She had hated it, or so she kept telling herself.

Life was better now. She dressed in comfortable clothing that gave her freedom of movement and—hallelujah— freedom from pantyhose. Work, although it didn't feel like work anymore, started when she arrived at the studio and ended when she left. She drank tea, meditated, and listened to soft music. Life was good. A little dull sometimes, but good.

Hailey glanced at the dashboard clock. She had enough time to stop by the motorcycle shop before getting back to the studio for her evening sessions.

She picked up her cell phone and plugged in the earpiece so she could drive and talk at the same time. She dialed her brother's number.

"You've got Jack," he answered.

"Tell me about it," Hailey said. "Very clever greeting. How old are you, anyway?"

"Thirty-two going on twelve," he said. "What can I do for you, sweetness?"

"I need to get a chopper donated for the Children's Hospital charity auction. Where should I go?"

"To church to pray," he said. "You really think you can get one of those donated?"

"Why not?" she asked. "It's a great cause."

"Sure it is, but you're not dealing with a corporation here," Jack said. "These are independently owned custom shops. These guys can't afford to give up a chopper just like that."

"I won't know until I ask, now will I?" she quipped.

"Uh-oh," he said. "You've got that determined sound in your voice. I haven't heard that since you left advertising."

"Here are my two options—I either get a chopper donated or I'm back on invitations. Let's just say I'm feeling very motivated."

"Got it," Jack said. "Poor bastard won't even know what hit him. There are two local shops. There's The Chop

Shop, where I bought my chopper. Kid Cassidy owns it. He's been in the biz for almost ten years and he's well respected in the chopper community, but he's tough. You're not going to be able to sweet-talk him. There's also J-Squared Choppers. I met Jim, the owner, and checked out his rep. He isn't so well respected. He uses cut-rate parts and charges high for them. I didn't trust him."

"Anyone else?" she asked.

"Yes, but you'd have to drive out of state."

"Then The Chop Shop it is," she said. "I'm on the Post Road headed east. How do I get there from here?"

"When you reach the center of Fairfield, look for the Cineplex and his shop one block down behind Hank's Diner. It's a five-bay garage. You can't miss it."

"Thanks, Jack. I'll see you at dinner next week."

"Hey, I have to ask," he said. "Have you told Mom yet?"

"About what?" she asked.

"The break up with Burke, quitting your job or opening a yoga studio?"

"Uh…no, no and no," she said. "I'm still waiting for the right time."

"Why do I think we'll all be dead by then?"

"Look, you're the golden boy. It's easy for you," Hailey said. "Mom thinks whatever you do is fine so long as you stay employed and don't bring home a prostitute as your wife. Me? Totally different expectations."

"That's because you've never told her where to put those expectations," he said.

"I just don't want to be held responsible when she has a stroke," Hailey said.

"She won't. Hailey, I know you want to make Mom happy, but you have to remember that she loves you and deep down she just wants you to be happy, too."

"And be married to a doctor, have two point five children and be a member of the most exclusive country club on the East Coast," she said. "Bleh."

"She only wants that for you because she has spent her whole life feeling excluded. In her own weird way, she is trying to protect you."

"Why doesn't she feel that way about you?" Hailey asked.

"Because I'm a man."

"That's so chauvinistic," Hailey protested.

"Mom's from the old country," he said. "You know how she is."

"Yeah, I know. I'll think about what you said."

"Good. And good luck with Kid."

"Kid," Hailey said aloud as she ended her cell phone call. "What kind of name is that, anyway?"

Despite Jack's negativity, she didn't imagine it could be too hard to get Kid Cassidy to donate a chopper to charity. The Children's Hospital was a terrific cause. Who could refuse?

The shop was located on a side street off Post Road in Fairfield, Connecticut. A huge sign perched over the top of a five-car garage announced that it was The Chop Shop. All of the bay doors were open and Hailey could see several men in work boots and blue coveralls milling around one of the bays.

She parked her Mercedes on the street in front of the diner next door. She stepped out of the car, smoothing her skirt as she walked. She took a moment to tug her jacket into place before approaching the garage.

The sound of someone hammering on metal rang through the street in an almost deafening pitch.

"Excuse me," she said, approaching the cluster of men. No one noticed her. She cleared her throat. "Excuse me."

No one could hear her over the banging. She sucked a deep breath into her lungs and shouted, "Excuse me!"

The banging stopped before she finished yelling and her voice echoed in the sudden silence of the concrete garage. *Figures,* she thought. She felt her face grow warm as all heads swiveled in her direction.

"If you're looking for the diner, it's next door," a terse voice said from amidst the group.

Hailey glanced at the motley crew in front of her and felt a shiver of unease prickle her. This was way more testosterone than she was used to confronting. Tattoos and earrings were in abundance. If she didn't know better, she'd think she had approached a chain gang. Jack had assured her that they were harmless. Yeah, they looked about as harmless as lifers in the pen.

"Well?" the voice spoke again.

"Actually, I'm looking for a Mr. Cassidy," she said. "Is he here?"

"You found him," the voice said as two of the men stepped aside.

Hailey saw a man in blue coveralls lying on a dolly beneath the bare steel frame of a motorcycle. The sleeves had been ripped off his coveralls, exposing muscled arms, one of which sported a wide Celtic tattoo around the bicep. He had jet-black hair cut in a choppy crew and he sported two small gold hoops in his left ear. Hailey thought he looked like a pirate. A slash of white teeth framed by a black goatee flashed at her.

"Taking inventory?" he asked.

"No, I...uh...that is..." Hailey stammered, embarrassed to have been caught staring. "Could I have a moment of your time, sir?"

He frowned at her. "That's one thing I don't have a lot of today."

The man rolled off the dolly in one graceful motion. Hailey found herself staring at the zipper on his coveralls.

Okay, so he was tall. Hailey tilted her head up and gave him her most winning smile.

"I'm not in sales," she said.

"Lady, you're all about selling something. Mortgage refinance, debt consolidation, encyclopedias, whatever," he said. "I'm sorry, but today is really not a good day."

Hailey frowned. Damn this suit. He was walking away, dismissing her. She hurried to follow him. The three men in their wake resumed banging on the motorcycle frame.

"Bidding is involved," she said, catching up to him before he disappeared into an office. "But it's for charity."

"Charity?" He gave a bewildered shake of his head. "If my luck doesn't change, I'm going to be the one who needs charity."

The office was enormous and decorated in early bachelor. Two brown leather couches and a matching chair circled a large-screen TV. Artwork of varying styles, but all featuring motorcycles graced the walls. At the end of the room were two other offices. Hailey followed him into the one that contained a beautiful cherry desk and several black leather chairs.

"Mr. Cassidy," Hailey tried again. "I think we've gotten off track. I'm here on behalf of the auction committee to raise funds for the Fairfield County Children's Hospital—"

"How much?" he interrupted her. He went behind the desk and flipped open a checkbook.

"Pardon?" she asked.

"How much do you want?" he repeated with barely concealed impatience.

"Oh, no," she said. "I'm not here for a donation. I was…that is…the committee…you see…"

"The point, lady," he sighed. "Get to the point."

"Would you consider donating a motorcycle for the silent auction?" she asked in one breath.

"Would I...are you...you're joking?" He leaned one hip on his desk and studied her as if he was sure she was crackers.

"I'm not," she said. "We need a good item for the silent auction and I believe one of your bikes would be just the thing."

He rubbed his temples and shook his head. "This day just keeps getting more and more bizarre. I'm sorry, but it's out of the question."

"But why?" she asked. This was such a good cause. How could he refuse?

"Let's see," he said, drawing her gaze up to his narrowed blue eyes. "Do you have any idea what one of these choppers costs?"

Hailey shook her head.

"A cheap one goes for fifty thousand," he said. "They're custom built for the owner, right down to the last nut and bolt."

"Wow." Hailey whistled. "I bet we could get at least one hundred fifty thousand at auction. That would make it the biggest-grossing auction ever."

"You're not hearing me, lady. There isn't going to be a bike in the auction. My business manager just ran off with my office manager and the bank has frozen all of my assets until we get this mess straightened out. Most of my existing contracts canceled when they heard what happened and have taken their business elsewhere. I'll be lucky if I'm still in business at the end of the month." He turned and stomped back into the garage.

Hailey watched him go with a frown. She should have called first. But she couldn't fail to get the chopper for the auction, otherwise she'd be demoted back to invitation stuffing again and then she'd have to slit her throat with an envelope because she just couldn't bear it.

"Mr. Cassidy," she called after him as she hurried across the garage in his wake. "I'm sure if you would just consider the benefits for a moment—"

"Look, Peaches," he interrupted her. "I'll cut you a check as a donation, although my apologies in advance for when it bounces, which it probably will. But I can't donate one of my choppers. First off, I don't have a spare one to give you and second, I've got to spend my time seeing if I can go out and drum up new business. And, by the way, no one calls me Mr. Cassidy but my accountant. The name is Kid."

"All right, Kid," she continued as if he hadn't said no. "Just consider that it could be a tax write-off for you, both the parts and the labor. And the name is Hailey."

"Well, Hailey, you look like a giant peach or maybe a kumquat in that suit," he said, looking her over from head to toe. "No offense, but that's really not your color. I see you as more of a purple sort of girl."

"Purple?" she repeated. He was knocking her off balance, making her lose her conversational footing. It was very hard to charm a client when you weren't prepared. Then it hit her. If she treated Kid Cassidy as a client and helped him with his business then maybe he would agree to help her.

"I think I can help you," she said.

"Good at filing and selling choppers, are you?" he asked with an almost smile.

"Give me twenty-four hours," she said.

"Yeah, sure," he said. The skepticism in his voice made it clear he didn't think he'd be seeing her again.

Hailey felt all of her old creative juices flowing. She'd come up with a plan that would knock his coveralls off. She grinned.

"See you soon," she said and hurried to her car.

Kid Cassidy watched the woman duck into her Mercedes and speed away. He was impressed with her ability to sprint in heels. He'd been even more impressed by the nice length of leg she'd been showing off.

"Well, that is surely a first, Kid," said Uncle Pete. "I've seen hundreds of women run after you, but I don't recall ever seeing one run away."

Kid glanced at the old man standing beside him. Uncle Pete was short and stocky with a thatch of white hair that refused to be combed down. No one knew exactly how old he was, not even Uncle Pete, but even his wrinkles had wrinkles.

Uncle Pete wasn't a blood relation, but that didn't lessen the bond between them. He had taken Kid under his wing when Kid had been a rebellious teenager headed for no good. Uncle Pete had taught him everything there was to know about motorcycles. It was a debt Kid would never be able to repay.

He shrugged at Pete. "Maybe I'm losing my charm."

"Ha!" Pete snorted. "What charm? Maybe you just met your match."

"Match? Peaches?" Kid pointed in the direction that the woman had fled. "Did you get a good look at her? She was corporate personified. She actually wanted me to donate a chopper, a freaking chopper. Believe me, me and Peaches have nothing in common."

"You gonna do it?" Pete asked.

"Hell, no. I don't have the time," Kid said. "Or the man power. Or the chopper."

"You'd best keep practicing saying that, then," Pete said. "Because mark my words, she'll be back."

"I don't think so," Kid said.

"I'll bet you a fifty on it," Pete said, looking confident.

"You're on," Kid agreed and shook his hand.

Pete shuffled away laughing.

Kid frowned out at the street. She wouldn't be back. He'd bet his license on it.

2

IF SHE COULD REACH HER backside with her foot, Hailey would kick herself all the way back to the studio. She supposed that she could give herself a good wallop if she assumed the *vrksasana*, also known as the tree pose, but that would probably look silly and she might fall and hurt herself.

Hailey frowned. She'd blown it. She knew better than to show up unprepared. She should have done more research, found an angle to work. What had she been thinking? She had thought this would be easy. How was she supposed to know that his business manager had run off with his secretary? She should have called. Maybe if he spent a day or two thinking about it, the idea of donating a motorcycle would be more appealing to him. Yeah, right.

She parked outside the yoga studio and hurried into the modest brick building. The yoga studio shared a building with Only Organic, a health-food store. When Madeline and Hailey had shopped for a building to buy, Hailey had chosen this one specifically because she'd hoped the proximity to the health-food store would cause a steady trickle of business for them. Her idea had paid off. Stressed-out commuters in and out of Manhattan flocked to their classes before picking up green tea and sprout dinners on the way home to their affluent Connecticut neighborhoods. The yoga business was booming.

Their studio contained one large mirrored room for

classes, two small meditation rooms and one office that they shared. The rear entrance to the studio opened into their office, and it was this entrance Hailey used, hoping to avoid being seen in her hideous suit. No such luck.

"Jeez, they couldn't even unload that thing at Goodwill?" Madeline asked. "I was sure someone would have snatched it up for a costume party. They could go as poor taste and their date could go as the fashion police."

"Contain yourself," Hailey said.

"I can't help it if I have a terrific imagination." Madeline shrugged and tossed her long black braid over her shoulder. "So how was lunch?"

"Miserable. Watercress sandwiches and weak tea."

"Bleck," they said together.

"And it only went downhill from there." Hailey kicked off her pumps and sank into the chair behind her desk. "I got volunteered to acquire the big-ticket item for this year's silent auction."

"Doesn't that beat licking, what, like three hundred and fifty envelopes?" Madeline asked.

"Yes, but the man I went to see about donating the motorcycle isn't interested and won't budge," Hailey said. "He's having a crisis."

"Go someplace else," Madeline said.

"There is no place else. The only other local guy is cut-rate, and that won't do."

Madeline climbed onto the empty desk across from Hailey's and sat with her feet tucked up onto her thighs in the lotus position. "Motorcycle guy, eh? Was he hot? Motorcycle guys are babes."

"Since when?" Hailey asked dubiously.

She watched as Madeline arched her back like a cat. She was slight in stature and could bend in ways of which Hailey could only dream. She wore a tight purple sports bra and baggy, blue-and-black plaid flannel pajama bottoms. Hailey glanced down at her orange suit and sighed. She had a feeling Kid Cassidy would have said yes to Madeline.

"He was, wasn't he?"

"What does that have to do with anything?" Hailey asked, trying not to think about Kid Cassidy and his black hair, big hands and wicked blue eyes.

"Because when it comes to hot men, you flirt about as well as a fly stuck in a plate of tuna salad."

"I wasn't there to flirt," Hailey protested.

"Yes, you were," Madeline said. "You have to use a little charm to get what you want."

"No, you have to make your client believe in you," Hailey said. "You have to make them believe in the profit."

"Phooey. This isn't an ad campaign," Madeline said. "You hide behind demographics and marketing lingo because hot men are out of your comfort zone."

"They are not. I am very comfortable with hot men. I have a terrific relationship with my brother Jack, and he's hot."

"Yes, he is and he's your brother," Madeline said. "That makes him null and void for this argument."

"I was comfortable with my clients."

"That's because you saw them as clients and not men," Madeline said. "Name one hot guy you've interacted with since we left New York."

"I'm comfortable with the mailman, and he's sort of cute," Hailey said.

"He's sixty-five and smells like onions. Try again."

"I have nice chats with the produce guy at Only Organic," Hailey said.

"The guy with the back hair and buckteeth?" Madeline asked. "Honey, you have got to get out more."

"How about Burke? He was hot," Hailey said.

"Yes, and you dated for six months before he slunk off to Boston—a fact, by the way, you still need to share with your mother."

Hailey sighed. "You're right. I am uncomfortable with hot men. I try but it's much more complicated than planning an ad campaign. There, you have market research and consumer trends to fall back on."

"Well, get over it. If you want this guy to make this donation then you need to charm him. You can start by losing the suit," Madeline said. "Go back to his garage tomorrow and don't leave until you get him to give you what you want."

Hailey felt her face flush and Madeline laughed. "So, he's that hot, eh?"

"Ugh!" Hailey said and laid her head on her desk.

HAILEY STOOD IN FRONT OF HER closet and frowned. She had never really noticed before how compartmentalized her life was. It all stared back at her from the recesses of her closet. There was the dutiful-daughter section, also known as the butt-ugly clothes from Mom. There was the corporate section from her ad days that she had weeded down to several gorgeous dark-toned suits. And finally, there was the new-Hailey section, the yoga teacher. It was all cotton and comfy, not exactly charm-a-man wear.

She blew an exasperated breath. She knew the drill. The longer she stood here, the more indecisive she'd become. Damn. Of all days, why was she having a "you are what you wear" fashion crisis today?

Because of him. It wasn't that she cared what he thought of her, she told herself, it was just that she didn't want him to call her Peaches again.

Hailey flipped through the hangers. It was very discouraging. If only she'd bought that low-cut, purple sweater she'd been eyeing at Neiman Marcus. Kid had said he could see her in purple, and it made her wonder if he'd notice. She scanned her closet. Not a lick of purple hanging anywhere.

She reached toward the back of her closet and found a pair of beige linen slacks. When all else failed, go for neutral. Paired with a light blue dress shirt and brown loafers, she looked casual but tidy. Very Kate Hepburn, she thought. She added a simple strand of pearls about her throat, hoping to soften her appearance. She debated wearing her hair down, but after years of wearing it in a twist, she wasn't comfortable any other way.

On the drive to The Chop Shop, Hailey treated herself to a grande café mocha from Starbucks. If Mr. Cassidy hadn't had a change of heart then she was going to have to talk him into it.

She knew she could do it. She'd been able to talk clients into taking much bigger risks than this. But she was going to have to tap into her old ad-exec personality. She suspected it was going to hurt. Like an unused muscle, she was afraid her skills may have atrophied.

"Maybe I should have had a martini instead of coffee," she muttered as she stepped out of her car. "Maybe then this would be easy."

She threw back her shoulders and strode toward the garage with a determined air. So what if she was faking it? She would talk Mr. Cassidy into this donation if it took her all day.

A sudden *vroom* to her left made her jump, and Hailey froze in midstep. Bearing down upon her in a flash of silver and black was the largest motorcycle she'd ever seen.

"Lady! Get out of the way!" one of the mechanics yelled from the garage.

Hailey stood immobile, as if caught in a trance, as her gaze took in the sight of Kid Cassidy astride the behemoth machine. He wore black cowboy boots, blue jeans and a white T-shirt that had a smear of grease across one sleeve. A black half helmet covered his head and dark sunglasses hid his eyes, but his black goatee framed the curve of his lips which parted in a smile.

The motorcycle roared to a stop right in front of her, just missing the toes of her sensible brown loafers by inches.

Hailey felt her heart dislodge itself from her throat and plummet back into her chest with a thunk. She planted her hands on her hips.

"Are you nuts?" she shouted. "You almost ran me over. You could have killed me!"

He cut the engine and her outraged shriek echoed in the parking lot. Hailey felt her stress level begin to rise to the boiling point and she was afraid her anxiety ulcers would start to riot.

She plunked down onto the asphalt and crossed her legs. She placed her hands palm up on her thighs, closed her eyes and began to make long *om* noises and she could feel the blood slowly recede from her temples. It appeared her head wouldn't explode at this moment.

When she opened her eyes, Kid was watching her with his head cocked to the side, like a dog hearing a high-pitched whistle.

"I have a plan," she said as she rose and brushed the dirt off the seat of her pants. "I can help you get your clients back, and more."

He quirked an eyebrow at her.

"I'm very good at…sales," she said. She refused to tell him about her success in advertising. She did not want Kid Cassidy associating that jingle with her.

"What do you know about choppers?" he asked.

"Nothing," she admitted. "But that doesn't matter. Look, my brother Jack recommended you to me. He bought a chopper from you about two years ago."

"Jack?"

"Fitzwilly," she said.

"Oh, Jack." He grinned. "The dot-com millionaire. How's his ride?"

"Sweet," she said. "He's taken me on a few rides. It's a great bike."

Kid inclined his head in thanks. Okay, flattery was working, Hailey thought. Now she had him where she wanted him.

"Kid Cassidy, I want to talk to you!" A woman in a pink bathrobe and matching fuzzy slippers was marching across the lot in their direction. She was sporting a serious case of bed head and carrying a box of chocolate cupcakes under her arm like a weapon. A ring of chocolate circled her mouth, which opened to shriek again.

Kid lifted a helmet off the back of the bike and tossed it at Hailey.

"Get on," he ordered.

Hailey didn't need to be told twice. She yanked the helmet on and scrambled up behind Kid. She grabbed him about the waist just as he revved the engine, sending them careening out of the parking lot and onto Post Road. Hailey glanced behind them to see the outraged woman in pink shouting after them as she jammed another cupcake into her mouth. Yikes.

They stopped at a red light and Kid turned around to face her.

"So, let me guess," she said. "Ex-girlfriend?"

"Hell, no," he said, looking horrified at the idea. "Try my business partner's pissed-off wife."

"Oh." Hailey winced. "You're the whipping boy?"

"Apparently," he said. "So, having fun yet?"

"Actually, yes," she said.

He looked surprised and then a slow smile spread across his features. Too bad he wasn't a model, Hailey thought, because that smile could sell anything.

When the light changed, Kid turned down an old postal route that led through an apple orchard. The trees were just beginning to blossom and Hailey felt herself smile. As the wind whipped by and the ground below them flew past in a blur, she felt as if she were flying.

They left the orchard behind and crossed over a set of railroad tracks, broke through some trees and found themselves on a short beach nestled between a marsh and a small bay.

Kid switched off the engine and put down the kickstand. He slid off the bike in one fluid motion. Hailey was not nearly so graceful. Her knees were cramped from being clenched around the bike in an unfamiliar grip, and instead of sliding off the seat, she rolled off and staggered in a futile attempt to keep her balance.

Kid looked at her with pity and steadied her with his hand.

"You okay?" he asked.

"Fine. Good. Great," she said as she tried not to lean too heavily upon him. "Don't I look it?"

"No," he answered. "You look like you're dressed for a croquet match not a ride on a motorcycle."

"My grandmother happens to think croquet is a blood sport, and she'd wipe up the court with you. Besides, I didn't know when I got up this morning that I would be taking a ride on a motorcycle."

"Next time, I'll call your social secretary in advance," he said. "You'd look pretty hot in some black leather pants, Peaches."

Hailey felt her face grow warm and she frowned at him. "My name is Hailey."

"Peaches suits you better," he said.

"Did you build this chopper?" she asked, wanting to change the subject

"No, this is my Harley." He pointed to the Harley-Davidson logo on the side of the bike. "I laid it down a few weeks ago and had to replace some parts. I'm giving it a test drive."

"Oh," Hailey said, barely resisting the urge to thunk her forehead with her palm. She should have noticed the logo. Argh. "Well, thank you for the ride, Mr. Cassidy."

"Everyone calls me Kid," he said.

"How'd you get that clunker of a nickname?" she asked. Oh, man, where was her brain? That sounded like an insult and here she was trying to be nice. Focus, Hailey, focus. She curved her lips into a maniacal smile so that he'd know she'd meant no offense.

"Don't strain yourself," he said with a laugh. "I'm not offended. When I was a teenager, I was in trouble quite a bit so I got the nickname Billy the Kid. The 'Kid' part stuck."

"So your given name is William?" she asked, placing her helmet beside his. Her hair fell down across her shoulders and she reached into it, searching for pins, but found none. They must've fallen out of her hair during the ride.

"Yeah, but no one calls me that except my mother, and that's only when she's sore at me," he noted.

She tucked her hair behind her ears, but it fell forward into her face. She tried to knot it at the nape of her neck, but it unraveled, causing her to sigh in exasperation.

Kid reached into his back pocket and pulled out a bandanna. "Here. You can tie your hair back with this."

It was navy-blue and white and appeared to be clean. She tried tying it around her hair, but it slid free.

Kid shook his head and said, "Peaches, you are not biker material."

"Sure I am," she said, tugging the bandanna so tight it smarted. "Ouch."

"Here, let me, before you hurt yourself," he said and took the bandanna from her.

He folded it into a large triangle and gently put it on her head, reaching around her neck to tie the corners underneath her hair. Hailey tried not to notice how gentle his fingers were when they brushed her skin or how solid his chest was. She had to resist the urge to lean into him. He smelled of gasoline and aftershave and soap. Hailey liked it. She liked it a lot.

Think ad campaign, she told herself. How could she use this?

Kid stepped away.

"Thank you, Mr…uh…Kid," Hailey stammered and then paused. She considered him for a moment. "It suits you."

"What does?" he asked.

"The nickname. You look like an outlaw."

"Does that make you nervous?" he asked. His blue eyes darkened wickedly and Hailey felt a shiver tingle the base of her spine. He was playing with her and she was enjoying it.

"Should it?" If she didn't know better, she'd think she was flirting.

He stepped toward her and fingered one of her curls. "Perhaps."

Hailey felt a prickle of heat coil around her. Oh, man, she was flirting and so was he!

"Come on," he said. He began to stride down the beach, giving Hailey little choice but to follow.

"Um…Kid, where are we going?" she asked, hopping in a futile attempt to keep sand from pouring into her loafers.

"You'll see." He climbed up a rock wall and turned to pull Hailey up behind him. His palm was rough with calluses and dwarfed Hailey's palm.

She tried to ignore the sizzling heat she felt radiating from him. She was here for charity, nothing more. She didn't care how fine his ass looked in a pair of 501s or how impossibly rock hard his shoulders appeared beneath his simple white cotton T-shirt. Really, she didn't.

She glanced around, noting that they were in a small boatyard, and she took a step to follow Kid, but it felt as if she were walking on sandpaper. She paused to pour the sand out of her loafers. Kid watched and shook his head. He led her down a long wooden dock toward a red shack that sat perched on the dock's edge.

"Aren't you worried about your Harley?"

"No," he said.

"But we just left it. What if—" she began to say, but he took her elbow and steered her toward the shack. The smell of fried fish greeted her nostrils and Hailey felt her stomach growl.

The shack was a restaurant. The Crab Shack. Hailey blinked in surprise. Large shutters opened to reveal a small kitchen and an open-air eating area full of weather-worn picnic tables that reached the end of the pier.

"What'll you have?" Kid asked.

"Are you serious?"

"Yeah. I dragged you out on this test drive. The least I can do is feed you."

"Well, in that case," she said, "I'd love some clam fritters, clam chowder, a lobster roll. Oh, and a beer, please—something light."

"Is that all?" he asked, clearly amused.

"Unless they have chocolate cupcakes," she teased.

"Sorry, fresh out," he answered drily and went to the counter to order.

The two men working behind the counter greeted him by name and the three of them began to chat. Hailey pretended not to notice when they glanced at her. It was obvious that they were checking her out. She kept her gaze focused on the water and listened to the soft slap of the waves against the wooden pilings.

She brushed some imaginary lint off her sleeve and took the opportunity to glance at the men with Kid. She wondered what sort of girl Kid usually brought down here—probably some Harley mama who packed weapons and knew how to tie her own bandanna. Hailey sighed. She wasn't even sure she liked Kid, so why did she care who hung on to the back of his motorcycle?

She glanced at him as he threw back his head and laughed at something one of the men said. His teeth were white against his black goatee. His throat was long and the sound of his laugh was deep and genuine. It made her want to laugh in return. The man was a babe. She was so far out of his league, she might as well be chasing the king of a small, independent nation. Good thing this was strictly business.

Kid returned with a plastic tray weighed down with two bowls of chowder, a heaping pile of clam fritters, two lobster rolls and a platter of fish and chips. He handed her a beer and asked, "Do you need a glass?"

She'd been in advertising long enough to know that one always mimicked a client. It made them feel at ease and built a rapport.

He didn't have a glass, so she said, "No thanks."

His glance was mocking. Obviously, her tactic wasn't working. She went for blunt.

"You don't like me very much, do you?" she asked.

"It's not personal," he said, taking a bite of fish and washing it down with a sip of beer. "It's not you as much as your type."

"My type?" she repeated. "I'm not a type."

"Sure you are."

"Okay, what is my type?" she asked, knowing full well that this showed a singular lack of good judgment.

"Well-bred rich girl desperately seeking a doctor for a husband," he said.

Ouch! Hailey thought. The doctor crack hit a little too close to home, even if it was more her mother's idea than her own.

"My parents are well off," she conceded. "That doesn't mean I'm rich."

"Doesn't it?" he asked. "Do you think most twenty-five-year-old girls zip around in a Mercedes?"

"I'm twenty-nine," she corrected him, taking a bite out of a clam fritter. "And I earned that Mercedes."

"Doing what?" he asked in a voice ripe with doubt.

"High-priced hooker," she said, wanting to shock him. And really an ad exec was a prostitute of sorts. "You wouldn't believe what I had to do for that car. Let's just say I spent a lot of time on my…hey, are you all right?"

Kid was choking on a clam fritter. He hadn't turned blue yet, so Hailey thumped him on the back and handed him his beer.

"A hooker? You?" he said, gasping.

"High-end," Hailey confirmed with a nod. "Very exclusive clientele."

"Does Jack know?"

"Sure, he's my pimp."

She tried to remain expressionless but then ruined it by laughing. Kid watched her for a moment and then grinned.

Hailey sucked in a breath. Kid's smile was so enticing she wanted to skinny-dip in it. Okay, she wanted to skinny-dip with more than his smile. Hailey gave herself a mental slap. Concentrate.

"Seriously, I do volunteer at the Children's Hospital and I work on the auction every year."

"Ah, yes," he said. "The auction."

"Have you had a chance to think about what we discussed the other day?" she asked, bolstering her courage by finishing her beer in one swallow.

"I already gave you my answer," he said, finishing the last of his chowder.

"But this is for children," she protested. She saw where he was looking and snatched the last fritter before he could get it.

"I'll gladly make a donation, but I don't have time to build a chopper for you."

She opened her mouth, looking as if she wanted to argue. Kid waited for the harangue to start. Whether she believed it or not, he had met her type before. Upper-crust debutantes who thought the world was theirs for the taking. Not this time.

She frowned but said nothing. Kid thought she would have stamped her little leather loafers and demanded her way by now. This was the third time this afternoon that she had managed to surprise him. The first time was when he'd seen her in the parking lot, when he'd been so sure she'd never return. And the second time was when she'd climbed onto the back of his Harley without hesitation. Of course, Stan's wife, Irene, may have had something to do with that. Or maybe Peaches wasn't the cream puff he thought she was.

"You say you don't have the man power to build this chopper right now?"

"That's right," he agreed.

"Is there any way to fix that?" she asked.

"What are you going to do, become my business/office manager?" As soon as the question flew out of his mouth, Kid knew that was the solution. The surefire way to get rid of Peaches was to threaten her with a job she'd find beneath her.

She looked intrigued. Uh-oh. Kid decided to lay it on a little thicker.

"Well, that's the only way this is going to happen. You rack up sales for me and manage my office and I'll build your bike. Take it or leave it."

She considered his offer. She looked as if she wanted to kick sand at him. Then she stunned him for the fourth time that day.

"I'll take it."

3

SHE WAS BLUFFING. KID WAS sure of it. She had to be working an angle. He just had to figure out what it was.

"This means you'll have to report to the garage every day," he said. "There won't be time for manicures or shopping."

"I know," she said, chewing her lower lip thoughtfully. "Do you think we'll be able to get it done in a month?"

He shrugged. He could build a basic one in a week, not that it mattered. He was sure she'd run screaming from the garage at the first squirt of the grease gun.

"The auction is four weeks away," she said. "Can we get it done by then?"

"That depends on you, Peaches," he said. "You make some sales and get some money rolling in and, yeah, we'll get it done."

"I need to work out a new schedule with my partner."

"Partner?" he asked.

"All high-priced call girls have partners," she said.

Kid pursed his lips and studied her for a moment. There was no doubt that Peaches came from money. She'd acknowledged that her parents were wealthy, but she'd said she earned her Mercedes. Curious. He knew she was joking about being a call girl, but still, she'd gotten her pricey wheels somehow. He didn't see a wedding ring on her finger, so she must have a job of some sort.

Kid frowned. Peaches intrigued him. She seemed so demure, but there was a sensuality to the curve of her lips and a wicked sparkle in her eyes that belied her conservative exterior. She tempted him. He didn't like that. He had no time in his life right now for this.

"Let's go," he said, stepping back from the table.

"Wait," she said and grabbed his arm. Kid studied her small hand on his forearm. Her touch was light and warm. "I'll report for work bright and early tomorrow morning. Do we have a deal?"

Kid looked at her in surprise. She was persistent. He had to give her that. He found himself shaking her hand, wondering if he'd just made a pact with the devil. Did the devil wear pressed slacks and cultured pearls? Apparently, this one did.

She wouldn't go through with it, he thought as they rode back through the orchard to the garage. What did she know about managing an office or selling choppers? She was catered luncheons and tennis lessons, not hydraulic lifts and hot wrenches. He'd humor her.

The truth was, the thought of having her around didn't bother him as much as it should have. He liked that she had spunk. She didn't back down easily. She was a real knockout when she let her hair down, and when she smiled her face lit up, making him want to smile in return. Yeah, he liked her way more than he should.

He tried not to notice the feel of her arms about his waist. She was soft against his back and her perfume was so faint he had to strain to get a whiff of it. It was feminine, like warm vanilla.

He supposed he should admire her motives to raise money for the Children's Hospital, but he didn't. So many of the social elite's causes were to better themselves that it was hard to say whether she was doing this for the right reasons or because she wanted to bag herself a cute doctor. Not that he cared, Kid reminded himself. He was sure she'd show up for a day or two, but the minute she got grease under her fingernails or in her hair, she'd be gone, baby, gone.

They roared into the parking lot of his five-bay garage. As soon as he switched off the engine, Uncle Pete was standing there with his hand out.

"I believe you owe me a fifty," he said with a grin.

Kid shrugged. "Take it out of petty cash, Uncle Pete. And while you're at it, find a pair of coveralls for Peaches here."

Uncle Pete's mouth formed a perfect O.

"My name is Hailey," she corrected him as she slid stiffly off the Harley and removed her helmet.

She held out her hand to Pete. A smudge of oil smeared her palm. Kid watched her. She didn't look offended or search for a hankie to wipe her hand on. Instead she smiled.

"Looks like I'd better get used to this."

"Oh, I'm sorry, miss," Uncle Pete said. "Let me get you a towel."

"Oh, no thank you," she said. She turned to Kid. "I can handle this if you can."

"We'll see, won't we?" he asked and watched her walk away.

Hailey sank into her blue Mercedes with a sigh. She'd done it. Kid Cassidy was going to donate a chopper to charity. Yes, she was going to have to help around the garage, but from an advertising standpoint it would make her job simpler. She'd have full access to her client. This could work. She was exhausted. She hadn't felt this tired since she had quit her job in Manhattan.

She wondered if Madeline was still at the studio. She could really use a martini and an evening of girl chat.

Hailey put her key in the ignition and started the car. The blue digital clock winked at her and she gasped. Six-thirty! Then she got that sick, feeling in her throat. It was Monday.

The first Monday of every month was the evening her family got together for dinner at the club. There was no excuse—except perhaps your own untimely demise—acceptable for not being in attendance. Punctuality and proper attire were vital, otherwise Selma would be displeased. And as Jack said, "When Selma ain't happy, ain't nobody happy."

Hailey felt herself break out into a nervous sweat.

She stomped on the gas pedal and floored it. She shot through downtown Fairfield and headed west toward Westport. If she hoofed it, she would only be ten minutes late. Not good but not a shooting offense, either.

Hailey pulled into the circular drive of the club. She hopped out of the car and tossed her keys at the waiting valet.

"Thanks, Andy," she said and ran past him and up the stairs into the club's main entrance hall.

Skidding to a stop in front of the French doors that led to the dining room, she tugged her shirt and pants into place, trying to smooth the creases from the afternoon's ride. She knew Selma would be displeased with the slacks, but it just couldn't be helped.

As she opened the massive doors and scuttled into the room, Beaumont, the club's maître d', watched her. He looked surprised. Hailey was sure he'd never seen her in slacks before. She sighed. If he'd reacted that badly then she could only imagine how Selma was going to react.

"Good evening, Miss Hailey." He tipped his head to her.

"Good evening, Beaumont," she returned. "I expect my family is waiting for me?"

"Most anxiously," he agreed. "Please follow me."

Candlelight, daffodils and crisp white linens decorated each table, giving the room an incandescent glow. They made their way across the floor to a table by the windows.

"Here you are, miss." Beaumont pulled out Hailey's chair and she sank gratefully into it.

"Hailey, where have you been?" Selma asked, leaning across the table. "I was beginning to worry."

"Hi, honey," her father said and kissed her cheek.

"Hi, Hail." Her brother Jack leaned in to kiss her other cheek. "This is a first. I was on time and you were late. Beaumont, would you have our waiter bring my sister a martini? I think she is going to need it."

"Make it a dirty one, please," Hailey said.

"One dirty martini coming up," Beaumont repeated and left.

"Hailey, you haven't answered my…" Selma trailed off and frowned. "What is that on your head?"

Hailey reached up and felt her hair. Uh-oh! The bandanna Kid had used to tie her hair back. She was still wearing it! She snatched it off her head.

"Uh…" Hailey didn't want to lie to her mother, but there was no way she could tell her the truth. Her mother would never approve.

"Well, I'm waiting," her mother snapped.

"I…uh…" Hailey stalled, hoping for a miraculous intervention or a fabulous lie to come to mind while her stomach knotted itself into a pretzel.

"It's a do-rag," Jack supplied.

"Do-rag?" Selma Fitzwilly's eyebrows rose up to her hairline. "What is that?"

"It's a biker term, as in hair*do* rag," Jack said. "So, did you get Kid to agree to donate a chopper?"

"Biker term? Who is Kid?" Their mother glanced between them with a frown.

"He's the guy I bought my chopper from," Jack said. "I told Hailey to go to him for a donation."

"Ugh. You know how I feel about that thing," Selma said with a sniff.

"Yes, Mother," Jack said and gave her a smacking kiss on the cheek. "You think it's juvenile and dangerous."

"Hailey, I had assumed that I would accompany you to acquire the motorcycle," Selma said with a frown.

Hailey had a vision of her mother meeting Kid Cassidy and she blanched. It would be sort of like Godzilla taking on King Kong. It was hard to say who would be the winner. Selma would demand a chopper and Kid would tell her to go to…well, it would be bad. Good thing she'd gone alone.

"Oh, well, I just dashed over there as a spur-of-the-moment kind of thing," she hedged.

"Did you get to try one out?" Jack asked. Hailey glared at him. He was not helping.

"Don't be ridiculous, Jack," Selma said. "Hailey is far too delicate to ride a motorcycle."

Hailey made bug eyes at her brother and he burst out laughing.

"Fun, was it?" he whispered. Hailey kicked him under the table and he yelped.

"Children, behave yourselves," Selma chastised them as if they were three instead of thirty.

"I apologize for being late," Hailey said.

"I trust it won't happen again. Also, if you are too pressed for time to go home and change before dinner then perhaps you should carry a change of clothing with you. The Thompsons are across the room, and I know that they play bridge with Burke's parents every week. I would hate for word to get back to them that he is dating a girl who doesn't know how to dress for dinner."

Hailey looked over her shoulder at the Thompsons. They were frowning at her. She gave them a little finger wave, which they ignored. Mercifully, Burke's parents were not with them. Selma's desire to move up the social ladder and into the club that Burke's parents belonged to was one of the many reasons that Hailey hadn't told her mother about her breakup with Burke. Okay, more accurately, her *dumping* by Burke—or rather by his housekeeper. Someday she really was going to have to break the news to her mother that she and Burke were no more. But not today.

"So, what's everyone having for dinner?" her father asked with a wink at Hailey. "I think I'm going to have the spareribs."

"Oh, no, dear, those are entirely too fatty," Selma said. "You should have the poached chicken."

Hailey sighed. Good old Dad. He always threw himself onto the fire when Selma's flames got too hot for Hailey to handle. She grabbed her dirty martini before the waiter even set it on the table.

"Hi, Jack." An adorable redhead wearing a backless dinner dress approached their table.

Hailey rolled her eyes. Jack was six foot three with black hair, golden eyes and dimples, and he was a self-made millionaire. Women did everything but throw room keys and panties at him when he walked into the room.

"Hi, Cherie," he said. "You remember my parents, John and Selma, and my sister Hailey."

"Of course," she said, pressing close to Jack and causing Selma to frown. "In fact, I heard Hailey was teaching yoga now and I was interested in taking classes so I could maintain my flexibility."

She arched her back, thrusting her breasts into Jack's face. He turned away from her and eyed Hailey. Obviously he thought this was a good segue into telling Selma about her new career. One look at Selma's frozen features and Hailey begged to differ. Her stomach clenched and she longed for a hit off a Maalox bottle.

"Oh, you must be mistaken," Selma said with a shake of her head. She fussed with the ruffles on her yellow-and-blue-striped blouse. "Hailey is in advertising. Why, she's won awards. She even designed that adult-diaper campaign with Kyle Weatherby. You know, 'Tinkle, Tinkle, I'm a Big Star.'"

As Selma sang, Hailey felt a pounding begin in her temples as her stomach folded itself into an accordion pleat. Selma was beaming with pride. How could she disappoint her? She gave Cherie a shrug and the girl wandered away, looking confused and embarrassed. At least Selma wound down before the second chorus. Thanks to Selma's enthusiasm, there wasn't a person in the tristate area who didn't know that Hailey had designed that campaign. She downed her martini in one swallow. So much for coming clean.

KID SAT AT HIS DESK AND retrieved his voice mail. Maybe Stan had called last night. No, but there were fifteen messages—all from Irene. Some were coherent but most were either drowned by tears or obscured by her yelling.

Kid let out a pent-up sigh. He had no idea what to do about Irene. He dialed Stan's cell again. There was no answer. Not a big surprise. He called the hotel where he suspected Stan was staying. They'd gone on a fishing trip to Belize two years before and Stan had loved it. The hotel staff refused to disturb Stan, and even Kid's bribes wouldn't work.

Kid glanced at his watch and frowned. It was seven-thirty. Where was Hailey? She hadn't even shown up for one day. She had seemed so earnest. Had he completely misjudged her?

She was probably still asleep in bed. Okay, bad idea to think about Hailey and bed at the same time. He shook his head. She probably thought that he'd started building the chopper already. Ha! Well, Peaches had a big disappointment awaiting her if and when she ever graced The Chop Shop with her presence.

Annoyed, Kid stomped into the garage. Why did he care whether she showed up or not? It was no skin off his nose, or any other body part for that matter. He had never wanted her here in the first place.

A blue Mercedes lurched to a stop in front of the garage. Hailey jumped out and raced toward the building.

"Sorry I'm late," she said. "There was an accident and the traffic was unbelievable."

Kid frowned. He'd felt a rush of something he refused to name at the sight of her. It was probably just gas, he told himself. He was definitely not happy to see her.

"I'll make the time up. I'll stay late."

"Then you'll be here alone," he said. "We close at four o'clock."

"I'll come in early tomorrow," she offered

Kid decided to take pity on her—this time.

"Let's just get to work," he said. "Why don't you go next door and order a half dozen cups of coffee to go. We're going to have a meeting in a half hour to go over all of our current projects."

"Shouldn't we talk about the chopper for the auction?" she asked.

"We will," he said and handed her a twenty.

"When?" she persisted.

Kid raised an eyebrow and studied her. "When I say so."

The expression on his face must have told her that this discussion was over. She reluctantly wandered over to the diner next door, glancing over her shoulder as she went.

"You're being kind of hard on her, don't you think?" Uncle Pete asked as he moved to stand beside him.

"No," Kid answered. "I'm not going to invest my time and money into a project only to have her flake out on me. We'll see how she does over the next couple of days."

"Going to try to drive her away, are you?" Pete asked.

Kid didn't answer.

"I bet you she sticks it out," Uncle Pete said.

"You really want to relieve your wallet of another Ben Franklin?"

"No, this is bigger than that," Uncle Pete said. "Loser rides down the Post Road in his tightie whities."

"You're just dying to get even for the time you lost the bet at the Orange County rally and had to ride around the fairgrounds in your BVDs," Kid said.

"Uh-huh," Pete agreed. "And now I have a sure thing."

"No way," Kid said. "By this time next week, she'll be history."

"You're on," Uncle Pete said and stuck out his hand.

Kid shook his hand. "I must be crazy. I bet we get fined for public indecency when your wrinkled carcass parades downtown."

Uncle Pete just laughed.

HAILEY WAS BEGINNING TO dislike Kid Cassidy. She'd spent the past four days schlepping donuts and coffee, filing invoices, answering the phone and being told to please stand out of the way. Convinced that each day would be different, she'd spent her nights reading up on motorcycles, the industry and tracking demographics, eagerly anticipating the day they began work on the chopper for charity. Well, so far Kid had done nothing but order her around. The only thing she'd really accomplished was cleaning the office and picking up his dry cleaning.

Why that man even had dry cleaning was beyond her. The only thing he ever wore was blue jeans and T-shirts. She refused to acknowledge how well he filled out those jeans and T-shirts. This was just business—or it would be if he would listen to her.

When she tried to propose an idea to help boost sales, he stalled her. When she asked about the chopper for charity, he was rendered stone-deaf.

Hailey stared at the enormous box of tools in front of her. Kid wanted them polished and inventoried. She didn't even know what half of these things were. Okay, she didn't know what *any* of these things were. She picked up a silver thingamajig that made a nice clicking sound when you spun the handle.

"That's a socket ratchet." Chooch, one of the mechanics, lumbered over to stand beside her. He picked up a small silver cylinder from the pile and attached it to the handle. "This is a five-sixteenths socket."

"I knew that," she said as she dumped it back in the box.

"Sure you did," he said. "And I bet you know what it's used for, too."

"Yep," Hailey lied.

She turned and glanced at the big man beside her. He was as tall as a small building and about as wide. He had a wild mane of frizzy brown hair that poked out from under his greasy Red Sox baseball hat. He had three days' worth of uneven stubble on his face, and when he chewed tobacco he made a sloshing noise out of the side of his mouth that sounded like "Chooch". That was how he'd gotten the nickname. Nasty habit aside, Hailey liked Chooch. His eyes crinkled in the corners when he laughed, and he laughed a lot.

"It's for knocking Kid Cassidy upside the head with if he stalls on my project anymore or gives me one more crummy chore to do," she said as she turned back to the miserable box of tools.

Chooch studied her for a moment. His eyes crinkled and he barked with laughter.

"I think you're going to have to come up with something better than that," Chooch said as his laughter subsided. "He's got a hard head."

"You're telling me, he says he wants me to help and be business/office manager, but every time I try to suggest something, he shoots it down."

"He thinks you're going to bail," Chooch said. "Remember, his business partner of five years just ran off and left him flat. He's not in a strong trust place right now."

"Strong trust place?" Hailey repeated. "Chooch, you sound like a woman."

"I'm in touch with my feminine side," he said and spit some tobacco into a paper cup. "The thing is, Kid doesn't think you could sell a canoe in a hundred-year flood."

"Are you kidding me?" she asked. "I could sell a freaking canoe in the desert."

"You're going to have to convince him."

"How?"

"Sell something," Chooch said.

"Then he'll…" Hailey began but Chooch was already walking away. Couldn't sell a canoe in a flood, eh?

She stomped through the break room, smiling tightly at the men as she passed. They were watching reruns of *Monster Garage* on the Discovery Channel while they enjoyed a coffee break, with their feet on the table and their hands in their pants Al Bundy, style. Ugh! Hailey kept going. She knocked once on Kid's door before flinging it wide open.

"Kid, we need to talk," she said.

Kid held up one hand as he was holding the phone with the other. Hailey shifted her weight from foot to foot. So much for her big entrance.

"Stan, call your wife. Today. I mean it. She's beginning to go sideways. And call me, too, while you're at it."

"Got a minute?" she asked.

"Huh," he grunted.

"Look, I feel that you are not taking my project very seriously. I would like to start work on the chopper for the auction today," she declared.

Kid made no comment.

"Kid?" she asked, stepping closer. "Did you hear a word I said?"

"Huh," he grunted again.

"Hey, anyone in there?" she asked as she waved a hand in front of his face.

"Oh, yeah," he said, blinking at her. "Here."

He handed her a twenty. "Go pick up some bagels, would you? I'm hungry today."

Hailey stared at him.

"What?" he asked.

"Nothing," she mumbled as she snatched the twenty, turned on her heel and slammed the door behind her.

She grabbed a file and her cell phone off of her desk, which sat in the corner of the break room, and managed to leave without kicking all of the guys' feet off the coffee table.

She stomped across the parking lot feeling defeated. What was wrong with her? Why couldn't she get her spiel out? She glanced down. It was the coveralls. They choked off her spin before she could get the words out.

Hailey stomped toward the diner, dialing as she walked. She needed professional help, and not of the therapeutic kind.

"I'm at Hank's Diner, on the corner of the Post Road and First Street, right next to The Chop Shop. Can you meet me? Bring the black suit I keep at the office. It's an emergency."

"Be there in ten minutes," Madeline said and hung up.

The diner boasted a long counter and several small tables and chairs. The tables were full so Hailey chose a seat at the counter.

"What'll it be?" Hank, the owner, asked. He was big, burly and bald. In the four days she'd been coming for coffee, she'd never seen him smile. Not once.

"A mallet to knock some sense into a fat head?" she asked.

"Sorry. Fresh out," he answered without so much as a smirk. "Coffee?"

"Please," Hailey said. Hank plopped a cup in front of her and turned back to the grill with a grunt. Hailey sighed. She couldn't even win a smile out of Hank.

"So, what's the emergency?" Madeline asked as she slid onto the stool beside Hailey. She had obviously just come from a class, as she was wearing a black sports bra and skintight leopard-print Lycra pants. Every eye in the diner was on Madeline.

She looked at Hailey and said, "Lovely outfit, by the way. When did you get released from the Big House?"

"Funny," Hailey said, looking down at her blue mechanic's attire. "I think it's another ploy by Kid to drive me away. Little does he know, I've been dealing with the fashion whims of Selma Fitzwilly all my life. It's ugly, but kinda comfy."

"So are potato sacks, but you don't wear them when you're trying to bend a man to your will. I can see why you need the suit."

"She's right," Hank chimed in from behind the counter and placed a cup of coffee in front of Madeline. "That's on the house, honey."

"Why, thank you," Madeline said and batted her eyelashes at him. Hank's entire head turned bright red and he grinned. Hailey thought he looked like a demonic radish.

"Don't mention it," he mumbled and walked away.

"How do you do that?" Hailey asked in bewilderment.

"It's a gift," Madeline answered. "Is it just me or are we out of our element here?"

Hailey glanced around the restaurant. Men in suits mingled with tradesmen in a sea of aftershave, sweat and a few serious cases of exposed butt crack.

"Maybe a little," she conceded. "Then again, if you were to pull your pants down in back..."

Madeline gave her a dark look.

"It was just a thought," she said. "Seriously, I need your help. Do you think you could look more secretarial?"

"Excuse me?" Madeline said. "I don't do secretarial."

"I have a plan to sell some choppers to dealerships," Hailey said. "It'll prove to Kid that I can drum up business, but it'll also give him some operating capital. But we need to look like successful businesswomen in order to pull it off."

"Bad plan, sis," a voice said as a man leaned in between them and kissed both of their cheeks.

"Jack, what are you doing here?" Hailey asked as she hugged him.

"Checking up on you, what else? Kid told me you were over here." He turned to Madeline and smiled. "Hi, Maddie."

Hailey was shocked to see her partner blush a lovely shade of pink. Nothing made Madeline blush, except perhaps her stallion of a brother. Interesting.

"If you're going to sell choppers, you need to know what you're talking about," he said. "I know you're a quick study, but do you really think you can pull it off?"

"I can…now that you're here," she said and looped an arm through his. "Advise me, oh captain of industry."

"First of all, lose the suit," he said. "That works in Manhattan, not here. You need to look like you can hold your own on a chopper if you're planning to sell them, even to a dealer."

"Check," Hailey said. "Madeline, where can I get biker threads?"

"My cousin has a secondhand shop around the corner," she said. "She can outfit you."

"Secondly, what sort of inventory does Kid have?"

"He works primarily on commission. That's why I was thinking if we sell a few on spec to a dealer, it gives him cash in hand and broadens his selling base."

"Good plan," Jack said. "Will he go for it?"

"I'll give it my best spin. The worst he can say is no," she said. Hailey opened the folder she had grabbed off her desk. "Check this out."

There were several professional photos of Kid's work. Mean-looking choppers that practically roared out of the frame. The last photo was of Kid. The photographer must have snapped it without Kid knowing. He was astride a behemoth cherry-red chopper with wide tires and gleaming chrome. The chopper was gorgeous, but it was Kid that drew the eye. There was a sheer, raw sex appeal about him that breathed slow and hot like a sleeping dragon.

"Whoa," Madeline coughed. "That could put a girl in a dead faint."

"Girl?" Jack snorted. "I'm a guy and I might faint."

Madeline burst into an uncharacteristic giggle and Hailey rolled her eyes.

"This is what's going to sell his choppers," she said. "Just one look at this photo and women will want to sleep with him and men will want to be him. I've already got a call in to the photographer to use it for an ad."

"Genius," Jack said.

"Yes, I am," Hailey agreed. "So, you want to come along and save my butt when they ask me about calipers or carburetors and I stand there stuttering like a fool?"

"Do I get to be the secretary and wear a skirt?" he asked.

"Micromini," Madeline said and looked pointedly at his butt. This time Jack blushed and Hailey thought she might really gack.

They walked three blocks past numerous red-brick buildings with white trim and charming old-fashioned lampposts. Finally, Madeline turned around the side of a building and walked down the alley. There was a side door built into the brick wall and she knocked.

"IRS, open up," she said.

"Very funny, cuz." The door opened and an older and more flamboyant version of Madeline—and that was saying something—was standing there.

"Charlotte, I have a fashion emergency," Madeline announced. "My friend here needs to look like a biker chick."

Charlotte stood aside and ushered them in. "Seems to me like that hideous sack she's wearing would be perfect for a biker."

"She needs to look like she's hanging off the back, not under it," Jack said.

"You're cute," Charlotte said, reaching out to squeeze his bicep. "I like you."

Madeline smacked her hand away. "Taken, for now."

"Fine," Charlotte said. "So, what do you have on under that rag?"

Hailey unzipped the coveralls and showed them her

plain white blouse, buttoned to the throat and neatly tucked into her navy linen slacks.

"What convent did you break out of?" Charlotte asked in bewilderment. "I thought you were a yoga teacher."

"I am," Hailey said.

"What do you…?"

"Don't even ask," Madeline said with a dramatic sigh. "Some days she shows up to teach looking as bundled up as a Sherpa leading an expedition up Mount Everest."

Charlotte shook her head. "What a waste. Or would that be what a *waist?*" Jack clapped a hand over his eyes as she tugged the coveralls off Hailey and studied her figure. "I think I have just the thing."

"See, I told you we'd take care of you," Madeline said and helped herself to a donut out of the box on her cousin's desk. Jack reached behind her and she slapped one into his hand.

Hailey watched Charlotte flit around the small store grabbing this and that, shaking her head and talking to herself. Circular racks were strategically placed around the room. A cart of refreshments sat between two cushy upholstered chairs. The shop had more of an exclusive boutique feel than that of a high end secondhand store. Hailey was impressed.

Charlotte came trotting back toward her and took her by the hand. "Go into the fitting room and try these on. I think I got your sizes right."

Hailey grabbed the armful of clothing before it fell on the floor. Charlotte pushed her into one of three small, curtained rooms and drew the curtain closed.

She quickly shed her clothes and pulled on the jeans. They were softly broken in and fit her perfectly. She turned in the mirror to catch the view from behind. *Would you look at that,* she thought, *I have a nice rear end.* She pulled on the shirt Charlotte had handed her. It was a formfitting paisley peasant top that was cut low enough in front to reveal a nice wedge of cleavage. The pale green fabric made her hair look red and her eyes golden. Wow. Lastly, she pulled on a pair of chunky black half boots that zipped on the inseam. These were butt-stomping boots if she'd ever seen them. She loved them!

Hailey pulled the pins out of her hair and let it fall around her shoulders in a mass of soft curls. She looked feisty and fiery and alive.

"Well?" Madeline hollered. "What's taking you so long? Let's see how you look."

Hailey stepped from behind the curtain. Both Madeline and Charlotte gasped. Jack grinned.

"I am good," Charlotte crowed. "No more mouse girl. Now you're ready to play with the big dogs. And Kid is the biggest dog of them all."

"Woof," Hailey barked and tossed her hair over her shoulder.

"That man isn't going to know what bit him," Madeline said.

"Or where," Charlotte added.

The cousins high-fived each other and Hailey laughed. Their enthusiasm was contagious.

4

"WE'LL TAKE THREE," THE MANAGER of the motorcycle dealership offered.

"Seven," Hailey countered. "And half up front and the
rest upon delivery."

"Four."

"Six."

"Five," he said.

"Done," Hailey said and stuck out her hand.

Norm Shanks grinned and clasped her hand in his.

"If you ever think about going into direct sales, call me
first."

Norm was fifty-something with thinning gray hair that
he had grown long and wore in a ponytail. He wore jeans,
cowboy boots and a leather vest over a dress shirt. He had
pictures of his grandkids and his wife on his desk. Hailey
liked him.

"I'll have my money guy draw up the papers and fax
them over to The Chop Shop," he said.

Hailey glanced at her watch. She'd have time to get to
the garage and talk to Kid first.

"Sounds great," she said. "We'll be in touch."

"Let me know when you get the ads ready," he said. "I'll
bankroll them if you put our logo on them, too."

"I like the way you're thinking, Norm," Hailey said
with a smile.

She left the office to find Jack and Madeline astride one of the showroom Harleys. Madeline was on back with her arms wrapped around Jack while he was making motor noises.

"Get down now," she hissed through her teeth. They hopped down and followed her out the door.

"How'd it go?" Jack asked.

"He's good for five," she said.

"Sweet," he said.

"Yeah, now I just have to tell Kid," Hailey said.

HAILEY MARCHED ACROSS THE parking lot. This was the moment of truth. She found Kid on a dolly under a motorcycle, only his boots and legs were visible.

Uncle Pete was squatting next to the engine, handing Kid tools. Hailey tapped him on the shoulder and put a finger to her lips. Uncle Pete took one look at her and his eyes bugged. With a grin, he swapped places with her.

"Screwdriver," Kid said from beneath the engine. Hailey glanced at the huge metal box beside her. The only screwdriver she'd ever seen had come in a rocks glass when her brother Jack ordered one at the country-club bar.

She grabbed the first thing she found and slapped it into Kid's extended palm with more force than was probably necessary.

"Ouch. Go easy, old man. No, no, no." Kid tossed the item aside. "I said a screwdriver, Uncle Pete."

Hailey glanced back at the metal box. She grabbed another item at random and slapped it into his hand.

"What the...?" Kid rolled out from under the engine and came face to cleavage with Hailey.

"I'm up here, Kid," she said and rose to a standing position.

"So I see," he said, rising to his feet.

"I need to talk to you."

"Uh-huh," Kid said, looking her over. "Shall we?"

Kid led the way into his office. *Just as well*, Hailey thought, as she followed. She'd rather he reamed her out of earshot of the rest of the garage.

"Nice outfit," he said. "You're really beginning to look the part."

Hailey couldn't tell if he was being sarcastic so she inclined her head and said nothing.

"I sold five choppers today."

"Pardon?" Kid froze with his butt halfway in his chair.

"Well, I did some research and there's a chopper outfit in the Midwest that managed to quadruple their sales volume in five years by going to the dealer. I've got a dealership that wants five for sure and another that's interested."

"They're buying on spec?" he asked.

"Custom choppers are hot," she said. "And they want in."

"We usually design for the buyer," he said, slowly lowering himself into his seat.

"Yes, but now you can build what you know works instead of spending time trying to talk a client into a specific rake or wheel," she said.

"Picked up on that, did you?" he asked.

"Hard to miss," she said.

"Got anything in writing?" he asked.

"Everything but the specific numbers," she said. "They will pay half up front and half on delivery, but I figured you'd better decide what half is."

Hailey didn't mention the ad campaign featuring Kid. Why bother him with details now?

"I get the feeling you're not telling me something," he said.

Hailey widened her eyes. "Me?"

Kid narrowed his gaze, then he smiled. "I don't care how you did it, you did great."

Hailey felt her spine collapse in relief and she got that buzz she always used to feel when a client liked her ideas. She tried to ignore it and sank into the chair opposite him.

"So, what kind of chopper did you have in mind for the auction?" he asked.

"What?" she asked.

"Come on," he said as he stood. "A deal's a deal."

Hailey followed him out of the office and back into the garage.

"Uncle Pete, Chooch, Mikey," Kid called.

The three men broke apart as if they hadn't been gossiping. Kid knew better. Most men were worse gossips than women, they just hid it behind a love of beer, sports and power tools.

"We're going to start building Peaches's chopper for charity today," he said. He ignored Uncle Pete and his gloating wide grin.

"Pay up!" Uncle Pete demanded.

"No," Kid said, giving him a warning glance.

"Oh, I think you should," Pete said with a snort.

Kid might have known he wouldn't let it lie.

"Pay up what?" Mikey asked, glancing between them.

Mikey was the youngest member of the Chop Shop team. His adoration and hero worship of Kid was obvious. He wore his light brown hair in the same style as Kid and was desperately trying to grow a similar goatee. It didn't appear to be in his genetic makeup, but that wasn't stopping him. Kid didn't mind. He only hoped he could be as good a role model to Mikey as Pete had been to him.

"Kid and I had a little wager," Uncle Pete said. "He lost."

"I'll pay up later," Kid said.

"No," Pete said with a shake of his head. "If I let you wait, you'll wait until dark. I think midday, when everyone can appreciate the view, is much more appropriate."

Chooch laughed. "Oh, no, not the Skivvies wager again."

"Oh, yeah," Uncle Pete said, doing a little dance of victory. He looked like a chicken with an egg stuck up its wazoo. "But this time Kid is going for a ride."

Kid heaved a beleaguered sigh. "Oh, all right, if we can get on with our day."

"Ha!" Uncle Pete crowed. "And no speeding. It's dangerous, and I want everyone to get a nice long look-see."

Kid began to unzip his coveralls and saw Hailey turn her head. Over her shoulder she asked, "What's going on?"

Chooch was laughing. Between guffaws he said, "Pete and Kid frequently wager the outcome of things like the Super Bowl, the World Series or who can belch the longest. You know, stuff like that."

"Very mature," she said.

"Yeah, well, betting for money can be boring, so the last time they had a big wager, the loser had to ride around the fairgrounds in his Skivvies. Pete lost and he's been waiting to get Kid back ever since."

"But you can't do that," Hailey said, spinning around to face Kid. "You'll get arrested!"

"Then you can come bail me out, because it's your fault," Kid said.

"My fault?" she asked.

Kid began to pull off his jeans. She yelped and spun back around and clapped a hand over her eyes.

"Yeah, who knew you would have such staying power," he said. "If you'd quit, like I figured, Uncle Pete would be making this ride now. Oh, well. Back in a flash. Pun intended."

"What?" she snapped. She turned around and glared at him. "You bet on me?"

KID WAS CLIMBING ONTO HIS chopper, oblivious to her outrage. He wore his boots, helmet and a pair of boxer shorts with Mickey Mouse heads all over them. Well, that certainly fit. Other than the Celtic band tattooed around his arm and a smaller one on his chest that she couldn't make out, he was completely naked.

She couldn't believe the jackass had bet that she would quit. It would serve him right if he did get arrested. With a wave, he zipped out of the yard and down the street.

The guys all ran hooting and hollering to the end of the lot to watch. Hailey trailed behind them. She couldn't believe she was entrusting her charity work to this bunch of overgrown adolescents. She saw Kid zip down the street without a backward glance. He should have looked ridiculous. Instead, he looked hot. She pulled her shirt away from her skin and tried to get some air.

Breathe, she told herself, *breathe. Think ad campaign.*

The sound of the chopper's motor faded and the men all turned back to the garage to resume their work. Hailey stood awkwardly in front of the garage. She wasn't sure what to do with herself, but she felt as if she ought to be doing something. None of the men offered any suggestions. She supposed she was sort of like the new kid at school. No one quite knew what to make of you and no one was going to get too close until they figured out whether you were a biter or not. She went into the office and looked to see if Norm's fax had arrived. It hadn't. Then she cleaned out the two items in her in-box.

The faint sound of a siren interspersed with the rumble of the returning chopper made Hailey hurry back outside. Kid roared into the lot with one of Fairfield's black-and-whites right behind him.

Hailey's eyes bugged. Kid was going to get arrested! This was not good. This was not going to help business at all. Maybe she could put a good spin on it, make the stunt one for charity or a clothing drive. Hey, there was an idea.

Kid sat astride the chopper and pulled off his helmet as a tall, lean police officer hopped out of the car and approached him. The officer didn't look very happy with Kid. Hailey wondered what kind of time a person had to do for riding a chopper in their underwear. She tried not to stare at Kid's muscle-hardened thigh.

"Are you crazy?" the officer yelled at Kid. "If you had wiped out, you would have left skin all over the pavement!"

"I was very careful," Kid replied. "I never even went over fifteen miles per hour. You should have heard the ladies honking at me."

He was talking back to the policeman. Was he insane?

"Yeah, they were honking because you looked like a dumbass and you were holding up traffic," the officer said.

Uncle Pete came to stand beside her. "Don't worry," he said. "That's Kid's older brother, Sam. He'll just yell at him like he always does."

"Kid has a brother?" she asked, noticing the resemblance for the first time.

"Yeah, Kid's the middle brother of the five Cassidy boys," Pete said.

"Five? Their poor mother," Hailey said. She could not fathom having five Kid Cassidys to contend with. She wasn't even managing one very well.

"Yeah, his father passed away right after his youngest

brother was born," Uncle Pete said. "It wasn't easy, but his mom turned out a fine batch of boys."

"Next time I see you pull a stunt like that, I will ticket you," Sam was saying. "I don't care what Mom says."

"Mom will probably write it herself." Kid laughed.

"You're right." Sam laughed in return. "She'll probably try to get me to enforce a time-out on you."

The two brothers chuckled and then thumped one another on the shoulder until they each winced and took a step away from each other, testosterone in action.

"Go get dressed," Sam said as he stepped back to his cruiser. "It's bad for my image as a badass law enforcer to be talking to an idiot in his underwear. And no more bets with Uncle Pete or I'll ticket you both."

Uncle Pete laughed and waved. "That'll be the day!"

Hailey watched Kid stroll toward the garage. He walked with the same casual grace that he moved with when fully dressed. She had to force her eyes away from his chest and his Mickey Mouse boxer shorts. She stared at the tips of his hair, afraid that if she looked any lower she wouldn't be able to stop herself from looking even lower.

Kid was pulling on his jeans, and this time Hailey did look lower—and she saw a heck of a lot more than Mickey Mouse. Her mouth popped open in surprise and Kid laughed as he fastened his jeans.

"Sorry about that," he said with a sheepish grin. "Looks like Mr. Happy was trying to make a break for it."

Hailey spun on her butt-stomping boot heel and turned her back to him. Her face felt as if it were on fire and she knew she must look like the typical shocked virgin. She wasn't, but…well, hell, how was she supposed to concentrate when she had seen more of Kid Cassidy than was even remotely decent? Especially when she wanted to see so much more?

"Come on, Peaches," Kid said. "We have work to do."

Hailey glanced over her shoulder. Kid was fully dressed and striding toward his office. He hadn't put his coveralls back on and she took a moment to appreciate his male form. He had broad shoulders which tapered to a trim waist. He was lean and long in all the right places and he had a nice backside. Hailey felt her face grow even hotter. Great! Now she was ogling him! There was something about Kid that brought her alarmingly in touch with her feminine side. She hoped like hell that it was a normal reaction and not just her, because she was going to market the hell out of him.

"Peaches!" he shouted from across the garage. "Are you coming or what?"

"The name is Hailey," she snapped, mad at him for making her ogle him and mad at herself for succumbing to the urge.

"Whatever," he drawled as he held open the office door for her. "Let's get to it."

She followed him into the office. He pulled a fax out of the machine and studied it. He frowned. He punched some numbers on his calculator and scribbled on the fax. Then he sent it back.

"We'll see if they go for it," he said.

"They will."

"You seem awfully confident."

"I am," she said.

"Good," he said. "We need to finish up our current project. I don't want us to distract the men anymore than we have today."

"Us?" she asked. "I'm a distraction?"

Kid looked at her across the desk and his gaze went right to her newly displayed cleavage. The tension between them crackled and Hailey finally shifted away from his gaze.

"Point made," she said.

Kid grinned. "Good, then let's get to work."

"Now?" she asked uncertain of this new and amazingly helpful Kid Cassidy.

"Yes, now," he said patiently. "Coffee?"

"Sure. Did you want me to make a pot or go next door to the diner?" she asked.

"Let me rephrase that," he said, looking chagrined as he lifted a pot from the coffeemaker behind his desk. "Would you like some coffee?"

"Why are you being so nice to me?" she asked suspiciously. "Because if you think that you can get rid of me by being nice, then you're wrong."

"Look, Peaches, uh, Hailey," he said, watching her from beneath his lashes. "I was wrong about you. Apparently you can be an office manager, business manager or frankly whatever you put your mind to. Like I said, a deal is a deal. You got us some operating capital and I'm going to build your chopper for charity."

"Is this an apology for treating me like a gofer?" she asked. He looked so damned uncomfortable that she had to smile.

"No," he denied and then relented. "Well, sort of."

"In that case, I accept," she said.

"Hmm," he grunted and opened up a pencil case. "Don't look so pleased with yourself. You have no idea the amount of work you have just let yourself in for."

HAILEY FELT DIZZY WHEN SHE arrived back at the studio that evening. She had spent three hours pouring over parts catalogs looking at things called "forks" and "fenders" and "tanks." She hadn't checked in the mirror, but she was pretty sure her eyes were spinning in circles in opposite directions. She felt as if she'd signed up for an immersion course in a foreign language and she was failing.

In the changing room, she switched from her new biker clothes to her yoga outfit. The office was separated from the studio by a large window; through it she could see Madeline leading a class through basic meditation. She pulled the purple batik curtain closed, blocking them from view. She needed peace. She needed quiet. Her cell phone rang. Naturally.

"Hello," Hailey said as she pushed the talk button and reclined into her desk chair.

"Hailey, this is your mother."

Hailey lurched upright, as if her mother would know she was slouching and correct her posture.

"The next meeting for the hospital auction is next week," Selma said. "What do you have to report?"

"Kid…Mr. Cassidy is going to donate one of his choppers," she said. It wasn't a total lie, she rationalized as her stomach gurgled with a wave of anxiety. There was no reason for her mother to know that she would be working there until it was built.

"Well, that's a relief. The committee will be very pleased, although I still don't like the idea. They're too dangerous. I really wish your brother would grow up and sell his."

Hailey closed her eyes. Now that Selma was wound up, it would be at least fifteen, maybe twenty, minutes before she was required to speak. She couldn't even imagine her mother's reaction if she found out Hailey was working in a garage. It would be slightly less terrifying than her mother's reaction if she knew Hailey had spent her day picturing Kid naked, in between reading parts catalogs.

What was she going to do? She couldn't be attracted to a man so totally not her type. She suspected he was the kind of man who didn't expect a woman's IQ to be higher than her bra size. Not that she wanted a chance with him, she told herself. Then she remembered her quick eyeful of Mr. Happy. Okay, maybe she did want just one chance with him—a one-nighter that would ruin her for the rest of her life, because no man would ever live up to him. Yeah, bad idea.

"Hailey, are you listening to me?" Selma snapped.

Hailey blinked. "Yes, Mother. Absolutely."

"Good," Selma said. "Then you can pick me up next week and we'll go to the meeting together."

"Uh, I don't know if I'll be able to get away from work," she said. She dreaded the thought of another stuffy luncheon.

"This is for charity," Selma said. "I'm sure they'll understand."

Hailey sighed. Her stomach hurt and she needed a drink. "I'll see you on Thursday, Mother."

"Don't be late this time," Selma said and hung up.

Hailey ended the call and practiced her breathing and chanted, "I am a river. I will go with the flow and stop trying to fight the current. I am a river."

"Uh-oh," Madeline said as she opened the office door. "Someone just got off the phone with her mother."

Hailey cracked one eyelid and looked at her. "How can you tell?"

"You're doing the 'I am a river' chant and you have that pinched look on your face like you just had your bikini hairs waxed."

"That bad?" Hailey asked.

"Yeah," Madeline said and draped a towel over her shoulders. "So, enough of Selma. How did the rest of your day go with Kid?"

"Fine," Hailey demurred. "He's finally taking me seriously."

"You should be taking him seriously," Madeline said and fanned herself with her hand. "He is *hot*."

"You think?" Hailey asked.

"Oh, puleeze." Madeline laughed at her. "You know it."

"I guess," Hailey said. "But I'm not his type. I'm pretty sure he goes for robust blondes, if you know what I mean."

"So what?" Madeline shrugged. "He's overdue for a lovely brunette, then."

"I cannot talk about this," she said. "Kid and I have a business relationship and that's it."

"Whatever," Madeline grumbled.

"So, what's going on with you and Jack?" she asked.

"Flirting for now," Madeline said. "But I'll keep you posted."

Hailey glanced at the clock. She couldn't resist teasing Madeline just a little. "It's time for my seniors' class. I think this whole thing with Kid would be easier to handle if I hadn't accidentally seen his wangdoodle, you know?"

"What?" Madeline's jaw dropped to her chest.

"You heard me," Hailey said with a grin as she hopped out of her chair and walked toward the door. "Oh, look, there are some of my students now. Gotta go."

"Don't you dare," Madeline said, but Hailey closed the door behind her. Madeline yanked it open. "I'll still be here after your class and I want full-frontal disclosure."

Hailey laughed as the door banged shut. It was fun to tease Madeline. Too bad she didn't really have a full-frontal story to share. It was more like a half-dressed Mr. Happy gone a-wandering. Judging by her reaction to that, she didn't know if she could handle a full-frontal anything with Kid. It made her warm just thinking about it.

"Hailey, stop thinking about sex and get over here," old Mrs. Witherspoon snapped as she bounced her cane off the floor. She was ninety if she was a day, and had the crotchety disposition to prove it.

"I was not…how could you…" Hailey stammered, nonplussed. "Mrs. Witherspoon!"

The white-haired old lady cackled with delight and

pointed a gnarled finger at her. "I knew it. Whenever Mr. Witherspoon was in the mood, he looked moony just like you're looking now. God rest his soul."

Hailey wondered if it was possible to die of embarrassment. She waited for a moment, but unfortunately, no, she didn't keel over on the spot.

"Bea, quit teasing her," Mrs. Compton chastised her friend. "You just ignore her, Hailey. Whatever you're thinking about is none of our business, even if it is sex."

Several gray and white heads in the class nodded in agreement.

Hailey forced her lips to curve up in a tight smile that felt more like a snarl. "Let's get started, shall we?"

She switched on the tape of nature sounds she used in class, but it didn't quite drown out the sound of laughter coming from the office or Mrs. Witherspoon's occasional snort.

"SO, WHAT DO YOU DO WHEN YOU'RE not here?" Uncle Pete asked Hailey as she unpacked the wheat-germ-and-sprout muffins that she had made the night before. It was early, and she and Pete were the first ones to arrive at The Chop Shop. Now that they were actually going to start building the chopper, she was eager to get started.

"Muffin?" she asked and held the plate out to Uncle Pete. His nose twitched suspiciously.

"They're good for you."

"That's the kiss of death," he grumped.

"Just take one and I'll tell you what I do," she said.

Pete snatched a muffin off the plate and took a bite. He didn't bother to hide his grimace. "It tastes like paste."

"Eat the whole thing," she said. "Or I won't tell you what I do."

Pete devoured it in three bites. "Spill it."

"Okay, but you can't tell Kid," she said.

"Tell Kid what?" Mikey asked as he and Chooch lumbered into the break room.

"Oh, no," Uncle Pete said. "You have to eat one of those healthy rocks. I'm not going to be the only one who suffers. Dang, I think I chipped a tooth."

Mikey and Chooch looked at the muffins with distaste.

"Eat 'em," Pete ordered. They choked them down.

"So, what's the secret?" Mikey asked.

"Uncle Pete asked me what I do when I'm not here," Hailey said. "I'll tell you, but you can't tell Kid."

"Why not?" Mikey asked.

"Because I told him I was a high-priced call girl," Hailey said.

The three men burst out laughing. And not little laughs, either. These were great big belly laughs. Hailey frowned.

"Easy, don't hurt yourselves," she said.

All three bowed their heads. One of them snorted, but Hailey couldn't tell who it was as they tried to stifle their laughter.

"I don't see what's so funny," she snapped.

"You? A call girl?" Mikey said, taking a gulp of air.

"You don't really think he believed you, do you?" Uncle Pete asked.

"Well, no, but… hey, I could be a call girl," she said.

The three of them busted up again. Hailey didn't know whether to be insulted or flattered. She was feeling a little of both.

"So what do you think I do?" she asked.

The three men settled down. Their laughter subsided and they began to study her.

"You're smart," Uncle Pete said. "I'm guessing you're a librarian. Yeah, I can see you with hair up, specs on your nose, saying, 'Shh.'"

"Yeah," Mikey agreed. "Either that or she's one of those museum types that knows about paintings and junk."

Great. Dull and duller, Hailey thought. That's how they saw her. Despite her love of libraries and museums, Hailey had no wish to be thought of as someone who spent her day shushing people, however inaccurate the stereotype was.

Chooch shook his head. "She's a yoga teacher, you dopes."

Hailey, Mikey and Pete stared at him wide eyed.

"How did you know?" she asked.

"The muffins clinched it," Chooch said. "But let's see…you have terrific posture, and I've seen you practice your *pranayama* breathing when Kid is annoying you. In fact, the day Kid almost ran you over with his Harley, you went right into the lotus position and began to chant. Your friend who was here yesterday is a walking poster child for a yoga teacher. What else could you be?"

Hailey stared at him as he packed a plug of chewing tobacco into his lip.

"How do you know so much about yoga?" she asked.

"I lived in the Far East for a few years," Chooch said.

"I didn't know that," Uncle Pete said.

"Me, neither," said Mikey.

"So much you don't know," Chooch said with a shake of his head and a teasing gleam in his eye. "Tomorrow, let's start our day with the sun salute. I'll meet you here at six-thirty."

"Okay," Hailey agreed. As the door shut behind him, she turned to Uncle Pete and Mikey and said, "He doesn't miss a thing, does he?"

"No, I don't," Kid said as he entered the break room. "Why are you three loitering around? We have work to do."

"Hailey brought muffins," Uncle Pete said. "Have one."

With a snort, he and Mikey disappeared into the garage. Kid looked at the plate. "Ick."

"They're good for you," Hailey said.

"So is abstinence, but you don't see me signing up for that," Kid said.

"I really wouldn't know, now would I?" she asked, turning away before he could answer. "Are we going to start the chopper today?"

"Actually, there's a rally this weekend that I need to get ready for," Kid said. "Why don't you start thinking about the parts we looked at yesterday and start making a list. Most of it I have here, but we'll need to go shopping at the warehouse to get the rest."

"What's a rally?" she asked.

"It's essentially a motorcycle convention," he said. "A great place to drum up business and usually score some more awards. I need to prove I'm still in the game without Stan as my front man."

He pointed a thumb in the direction of the far wall. It was filled to bursting with trophy cups and blue ribbons.

"What are those for?" Hailey asked.

"My choppers," he said with a wry twist of his lips. "Although, a few of them are my dad's. He passed away when I was a kid, but he built a few choppers in his time that were revolutionary. I still have them and the trophies he won with them."

"I'm sorry." Hailey looked at the wall again. Three of the smaller trophies gleamed in comparison to the others.

"So, you're carrying on his legacy?" she asked and he nodded. "Looks like you're doing pretty well."

"I like to think he'd be proud."

"My brother said you were the best," Hailey said as she approached the wall. "But I had no idea. We could use these awards to market you. You need a Web site."

"Stan and I talked about that," Kid said. "Oh, crap." He grabbed Hailey's arm and yanked her down to the floor.

"What the...?" she sputtered as he pushed her behind her desk.

"Shh," he said and then pointed to the window.

Hailey peeked behind the chair. Irene stood there in the same pink bathrobe and fuzzy slippers. Her bed head now looked as if it were home to a family of small animals and in her arms she clutched a bag of pork rinds.

She stepped over the shrubs in front of the office window and pressed herself against the glass.

"Eep," Hailey squeaked and pressed her face to the floor. "You should talk to her."

"I have," Kid said, his face just inches from hers. "Five times a day for over a week. I can't get a hold of Stan. This is a nightmare."

"Maybe I should talk to her," Hailey offered.

"Not in that," Kid said. "She'd eat you alive."

Hailey was wearing another pair of hip-hugging jeans and Madeline's dark blue T-shirt with a big Bazooka bubble-gum label across her chest that left two inches of her midriff bare. She felt ridiculous, but Madeline had sworn that the mix of an innocent bubble gum label clinging to womanly curves never failed to get her what she wanted. Hailey had worn it in case Kid waffled on the chopper.

Hailey was about to protest, but Irene abruptly stepped out of the shrubs and stormed back across the lot.

"I feel sorry for her," Hailey said as she rose.

"Every story has two sides," Kid said, following her.

Hailey looked at him but he didn't elaborate.

"She needs professional help," she said.

"Is that what you do?" he asked.

"What do you mean?"

"Are you a counselor?"

"What? You don't believe I'm a high-priced call girl?" she asked.

"Uh, no, I don't believe it," he said.

"Man, why doesn't anyone believe me? Am I just not hooker material?"

Kid stepped closer and looked her up and down. "I wouldn't know about that, now would I?" he asked.

The tension between them hummed and Hailey heard herself swallow. It sounded comically loud, and she wondered if he'd heard it, too. Kid was more man than she was accustomed to handling. She really was so much better at dealing with corporate men in Brooks Brothers suits and ties. So, what if they usually wore too much aftershave and lived on their cell phones? At least they didn't scare the pants off her.

Kid, on the other hand, made her worry that her pants would walk off on their own volition. How was a woman supposed to deal with that?

"What can I do to help get ready for the rally?" she asked, taking a step away from him and changing the subject. "When do we leave?"

"We?" he asked. "You're not going."

"Why not?" she asked.

"Because it's no place for…" he said, trailing off.

"For?" she prompted.

"You," he said.

"But why not?" she asked.

"It's just not your style," he said. He was moving towards the garage in an obvious effort to escape her.

"What do you know about my style?"

"Peaches, it's hard to miss." He paused to eyeball her shirt. "Even when you wear someone else's clothes, you're still a good girl. Besides, someone needs to stay and manage the office."

"Good girl? Why do I feel like that is just the hugest insult?" she asked, but the door shut behind Kid, blocking any answer he might have given her.

She glared at the trophy case and scowled. "Good thing he wins awards for choppers," she said out loud, "because his people skills stink."

She stomped into the utility closet next to the break room's one and only bathroom and grabbed a box of industrial-strength paper towels and a bottle of Windex, then set to work on Kid's trophies. Some people ate when they were mad; some people cried. Hailey cleaned.

She took out her cell phone and called her office while she swiped the dust and cobwebs off Kid's trophies.

"Talk to me," Madeline said when she answered.

"There's a motorcycle rally this weekend. Kid says someone needs to watch the office. He didn't say it had to be me. So, how would you feel about minding the office at The Chop Shop this weekend?" Hailey asked.

"Oh, a day of hot motorcycle guys?" Madeline said. "Sounds rough. Our trainee Gladys can cover the classes, so I think I can make it."

"Great. Now I just need Kid to fall in line," Hailey said. "If he pulls the plug on this project, my name is mud. And even worse, the kids lose out."

"Don't take no for an answer," Madeline said. "Keep buzzing around him in that shirt and I guarantee you he'll give in."

"What if he doesn't?" Hailey asked.

"He's a man," Madeline said. "He'll crack. Just don't let up. Make sure you and the shirt are underfoot all day."

"Me and Bazooka got it going on," Hailey promised and hung up.

Hailey mulled her strategy for the better part of an hour

while polishing the trophies and dusting the shelves. When she stepped back, it was as if someone had switched on a light. The trophies gleamed. Hailey narrowed her eyes at their brilliance.

"He doesn't know it yet, but I'm going to that rally," she said. "Even if I have to walk there."

"IS SHE STILL CLEANING?" KID asked Uncle Pete from his spot behind the supply shelves.

Pete craned his neck to see through the window from the garage. "No, she stopped. So, how long are you going to hide from her?"

"I'm not hiding," Kid said. "I'm just refusing to have an argument."

"Just let her go to the rally, then," Pete said. "What's the big deal?"

"It's not a big deal," Kid said. "I just don't want her to slow me down."

"Yeah," Uncle Pete nodded. "I can see how that would be a problem. Having a babe on your arm is a real drag, especially at a motorcycle expo."

"She's not a babe," Kid said.

Pete looked from him to the window. Kid followed the old man's gaze. Hailey was outlined in the light coming from his office. Her long, dark hair was loose and curled down her back in wild tendrils. Her T-shirt clung to her curves and revealed a nice wedge of bare skin. Her jeans rode erotically on her hips and she wore her butt-stomping boots, which added two inches to her height, making her almost tall.

Uncle Pete looked back at him and shook his head. "Yeah, she's a real dog. I can see why you might not want to be seen with her."

"You know what I mean," Kid said. "She's a knock out, but she doesn't fit in. Rallies can be wild."

"That's not fair to her," Uncle Pete said. "And I really hate to take your money, but I bet you a hundred bucks that she goes and has a great time."

"You really like being parted from your cash, don't you?"

"When it comes to her, I'm two for two."

"You should quit while you're ahead," Kid said.

"Oh, yeah? Well, brace yourself, big guy," Pete said. "Here she comes."

"Oh, crap." He glanced around looking for an escape, but he was surrounded by shelves. There was no way out.

5

"KID, I NEED TO TALK TO YOU," Hailey said as she marched across the garage.

"See ya," Uncle Pete said and ducked around Hailey to the safety of the garage.

"Did you decide what fork you want on that chopper?" Kid asked with a benign smile.

"No, but I think the rally will be a great place for me to see what's out there and then decide," she said and beamed at him. "As your business manager, I really need to see the competition."

Kid frowned. "We'll take pictures for you."

"No, I really think I need to be there. You know, to soak up the atmosphere and all. Besides, I found someone to watch the office while I'm away." She arched her back as she leaned against the shelves. Now she was playing hard-ball. Kid winced.

"You're just going to keep nagging me until I give in, aren't you?" he asked.

"That was the plan," she agreed.

"Okay, I have a deal for you," he said. "I'm going to ask you one very simple question and if you can answer it, you can go."

"Define simple," she said.

Kid was aware that Chooch and Mikey were watching them from where they were pounding a piece of sheet metal into the shape of an oblong bowl to be used as a tank. He thought about telling them to mind their own business, but he knew they'd just pretend to be working while they listened to every word that he and Hailey said.

"I can't define simple," he said. "I don't want to give away the answer."

"Why do I think you're going to ask me something about the internal combustion system that I have no chance in hell of answering?" she asked.

"Life is risks," he said with a shrug. "Answer the question correctly and you can go with us, get it wrong and you stay here—with no arguments."

Hailey twisted her fingers. Kid knew that she knew better than to trust him. But she was also sure that he would keep his promise. If she answered the question correctly, then she could go with his support. Not that he could really stop her if she decided she was going. But he was betting that she would honor the agreement. She tipped up her chin.

"What's the question?" she asked.

"What's this?" he asked as he grabbed a tool out of his tool box. It gleamed in the garage's fluorescent light from her recent polishing and sorting. A slow smile spread across her face.

"Why, I believe that's a five-sixteenths hex socket on a ratchet handle."

Kid shook his head. He must have heard her wrong.

"Again, please?"

Hailey looked over her shoulder at Chooch. He feigned a coughing fit, but Kid could tell by the twinkle in his eye that he was trying to hide his laughter.

"A five-sixteenths hex socket on a ratchet handle. The socket pops off like this," she said and took the ratchet from Kid's hands and twisted the socket off. "See?"

Kid lowered his head to the metal work shelf and banged it three times. Hard.

Hailey cringed and asked, "Does that mean I can go?"

"Fine," he said. A glance at his reflection in a rearview mirror lying on the shelf above him showed a big, red mark the size of a quarter was blossoming in the middle of his forehead. "You can go, but you ride with Chooch in the van."

Hailey opened her mouth to answer, but he interrupted. "No arguments."

"I was going to say thank you."

"Don't mention it." He scowled. The statement wasn't a social nicety as much as a threat.

"I promise," she said.

Hailey sidled away as if she were afraid Kid was going to whack his head hard enough to knock himself out. He thought the idea certainly had appeal. He'd never met a woman who had this sort of effect upon him before, the need to do himself injury. It couldn't be a good thing.

THE NEXT MORNING, HAILEY arrived at the garage before anyone else, partly because she was afraid that if she were late Kid would leave her behind and partly because she was excited to go.

She had already consulted Charlotte for the appropriate attire. She was wearing low-ride jeans and a red halter top, topped by a black leather jacket and of course her butt-stomping boots. Charlotte had also educated her in the fine art of do-rag tying and Hailey felt sure that if the need arose, she could do a decent job with her own black bandanna—not that she would mind if Kid felt the need to help her.

The sound of an engine roared and Hailey glanced up to see if it was Kid arriving. She felt a twitchy sort of nervousness bolt through her, but it disappeared when she recognized Chooch aboard his enormous electric-blue chopper. He stopped beside her and switched off the engine.

"You're early," he said.

"I was afraid of being left behind."

"Wise woman," he said with a nod. "How about an early morning sun salute?"

"Out here?" she asked.

"Why not? It's a beautiful day."

Why not indeed? The sun was just lightening the sky and warming the cool morning air. It would be good to relieve some of her stress with a basic stretch.

Chooch went and retrieved a blanket from the break room. Hailey slid out of her jacket and slipped off her boots. Together they stood on the blanket and closed their eyes in meditation.

"What are you doing?" Uncle Pete asked as he and Mikey strolled over from Hank's Diner, each with a steaming cup of coffee in hand.

"Sun salute," Chooch said without opening his eyes. Hailey snapped hers shut again.

"Ready?" he asked.

"Yes," she said.

In unison, they opened their eyes and, while exhaling, brought their hands together in front of their chests in the prayer position.

The sun salute, or *surya namaskar*, was comprised of twelve positions, and Hailey and Chooch moved through them together, from the arched back to the downward-facing dog and finally back to the prayer position.

Despite her concentration, Hailey couldn't help but notice that Chooch moved with considerable grace for such a large man. Apparently, Uncle Pete and Mikey couldn't believe it either as they both stood with their mouths agape as they watched.

"*Namaste,*" Chooch said and bowed to Hailey.

"*Namaste.*" Hailey returned the bow.

"That's cool," Mikey said. "What's it supposed to do for you?"

"What do you mean?" Chooch asked

"Does it buff up your pecs or abs?"

"It could," Hailey said. "Yoga is a workout that combines your mind and body. Here. Let me show you.

"This is the most basic pose. Stand with your feet parallel with your shoulders and close your eyes," Hailey said. Chooch took Mikey and Pete's coffee cups and they each mimicked her posture.

"Listen to your breathing," she said. "Be aware of how the air fills your lungs and the sound of your beating heart."

"This doesn't seem like much of a workout," Mikey said. "I feel like I'm going to sleep standing up."

"That's good," Hailey said. "You're relaxed."

"Can't we learn how to stand on our heads?" he asked.

"Uh, no thanks." Uncle Pete's eyes popped open and his jowls wobbled. "I figure if I was meant to stand on the top of my head, it would be flat."

Hailey laughed. "How about an *asana?*"

"A what?" Mikey asked.

"An *asana,*" Chooch repeated. "It's a series of moves that you go through. How about the tree?"

"Do you think they're ready?" Hailey asked.

"We'll do the beginner's version," Chooch said.

"All right, but if it hurts, tell me and we'll work your way out of it," Hailey said. Mikey and Pete exchanged a dubious look.

"Stand on one foot and place your other foot with toes

pointing to the ground on the inside of your knee," Hailey instructed as she placed her own foot on the inside of her knee. "Breathe and concentrate on your balance."

The three men followed her lead. Uncle Pete teetered to the side, but Chooch righted him before he wobbled over.

"Now hold your arms out to the side," Hailey said as she moved her arms out. "Remember to breathe through your movements. Don't hold your breath."

Mikey tottered on his feet, but Chooch spotted him, keeping him upright.

"Now stretch your arms up over your head," Hailey instructed.

Both men followed her lead.

"Look at me," Mikey said, "I'm doing it."

"Concentrate," Hailey said. "Keep breathing."

The roar of a motorcycle engine broke through the stillness of the morning. Kid's big, black machine lurched into the parking lot. He took one look at his mechanics and braked hard.

Mikey and Uncle Pete wobbled and tried to maintain their positions, but the moment was broken. Chooch caught them before they fell.

"What is this?" Kid barked as he switched off his engine.

"Yoga," said Hailey as she eased out of the *asana*.

"Pardon?" Kid blinked as he removed his half helmet.

"You should try it, boss," Mikey said. "Hailey's good."

Kid glared at him. Mikey and Pete picked up their shoes and coffee and scuttled into the garage.

"Yoga? You're teaching my mechanics yoga?" he snarled at Hailey.

"Actually, I'm already quite knowledgeable," Chooch said. Kid lowered one eyebrow in his direction. Chooch picked up his shoes and followed Mikey and Uncle Pete.

"What's wrong with yoga?" Hailey asked. "It's very healthy, a real de-stressor. You should try it."

"I wouldn't have any stress if…" Kid's words trailed off and Hailey prompted, "If what?"

"If certain charity do-gooders wouldn't show up at my shop wearing almost nothing and turning my guys into sissies."

"Ah!" Hailey's mouth popped open in outrage. "I'll have you know that yoga is not for sissies. It requires strength, coordination, balance and concentration."

"So does ballet, but you don't see any of these guys flitting around in tutus, do you?"

"That's the most narrow-minded argument I've ever heard," Hailey snapped. "I'll have you know Chooch has studied yoga on his own, long before I came here, and he's very good."

"He has?" Kid looked puzzled.

"So much you don't know," Hailey said and shook her head. She didn't care if she was just repeating Chooch's words or that she really didn't know as much about him as Kid did. She knew this, and it certainly made her sound as if she was winning the argument. Petty? Yes. But he deserved it. She put her hands on her hips and thrust out her chest to accentuate her argument. It backfired.

"You're enjoying this, aren't you?" he asked.

"No," she denied. "Okay, maybe a little."

"You're not wearing that to the rally," he said.

Hailey glanced down at her red hoochie-mama halter top.

"Yes, I am," she said.

"No, you're not," he said and walked into the garage.

"What do you mean I'm not?" she asked, following him. She had just cleared the doorway when a T-shirt smacked her upside the head.

"Everyone representing The Chop Shop at the rally

wears one of these," he said. "For publicity purposes. And as our business manager, I'm sure you understand."

Hailey held out the shirt. It was black, triple-XL, with The Chop Shop logo in orange. She could have fit three of her into it. She glanced up at Kid. He was smiling.

"Have anything in a medium?" she asked.

"No," he said. "Sorry."

He didn't look one bit sorry. How was she supposed to fit in at a biker rally when she looked as if she was going to be covered from head to foot? All she needed was some sensible shoes and a hat and she'd be as appealing as a knockwurst. Normally, she was fine with promoting the product no matter what, but today she wanted to be noticed. She wanted to know how it felt to have a man's appreciative gaze upon her. Okay, she specifically wanted to know what it was like to have *Kid's* appreciative gaze upon her, especially if she was going to be hanging around a bunch of hoochie-mama biker chicks. Dang!

"Okay, people, let's get ready to ride," Kid announced to the room.

Hailey pulled the T-shirt over her head. It came down to her knees and made her boobs—not the largest globes to begin with—look droopy. Great. She glanced up to find Kid smiling at her from across the room. She was going to get him for this.

THE RIDE TO THE RALLY TOOK about an hour. Hailey sat beside Chooch in the van. She was relieved to have a break from the tension with Kid. She watched him rev his chopper ahead of Mikey and Uncle Pete. The wind whipped at the leather jacket he wore and she remembered vividly the day he had taken her for a ride—her arms wrapped around his chest and the smell of him mingling with apple blossoms. It had been intoxicating.

Of course, nothing was ever going to happen between them. He thought she was a piece of fluff. A do-gooder with a big bank account who cared more about a shoe sale at Nordstrom than...well, shoe sales were important, but she was more than that. Not that she cared about his opinion of her. He was going to build the chopper and that was all that mattered.

"Chooch, how did you meet Kid?" she asked.

"Tattoo parlor," he said.

"Really?" she asked.

"Nah," he snorted. "It just sounds better than the truth."

"What's the truth?"

"We met at a plant nursery," he said. "We were both eyeing the same batch of purple pansies. Almost got into a brawl."

Hailey burst out laughing. "You're teasing me."

"Ask Kid," he said. "I gave him the pansies and he gave me a job."

"Unbelievable. So, what's your story, Chooch?" she asked. "Are you from here?"

"I'm from everywhere and nowhere," he said. "I've been on my own as long as I can remember. That makes it tough to put down roots."

"Ah." Hailey nodded. Chooch was obviously a private person. She could respect that. "So, do you think Stan will ever come back?"

"It has to run its course." Chooch shrugged. "Only Stan and Irene can know the outcome."

"You're very Zen-like," Hailey said.

"I had a lot of time in solitary to meditate," he said.

"Oh," Hailey said, hoping she didn't sound alarmed. Did he mean time in solitary as in prison, or time spent solitarily? Then again, maybe she really didn't want to know.

Chooch turned onto an exit and followed Kid and the

others along a winding road through Litchfield County. It was a beautiful day and Hailey rolled down her window to let the sweet morning air into the stuffy van.

Kid, Mikey and Uncle Pete parked their choppers all in a row. The atmosphere was electric as booths and vendors surrounded them, all making their last-minute preparations for the rally.

Hailey began to walk away from the tented plot that served as their spot, but Kid stopped her with a hand on her elbow.

"Where are you going?" he asked.

"I thought I'd look around."

"You can. After we set up."

"Oh, okay," she agreed. "What can I do to help?"

"Here," he said and handed her a bucket full of sudsy water and a big sponge. "You can wash the bug splatter off our choppers."

"Excuse me?" she asked.

"Well, you're here to help, right?" he asked, looking amused.

Hailey frowned. He had her there.

"Fine," she said and stomped toward the choppers.

"When you're done washing them, you can buff them with this." Kid tossed a soft blue cloth at her.

Hailey caught the cloth before it landed in the dirt and managed to slop only half of the soapy water onto her boots.

"Buff you," she muttered. Good thing she liked to clean when she was mad, because right now she was pretty pissed. When she got done with these choppers, they were going to sparkle and she was going to check out the rally.

Two hours later, she was buffing the last spoke when Kid reappeared. He was busily chatting with some half-naked woman wearing cutoff shorts that were cut so high the fleshy globes of her rear hung out the bottom. For a top, she had on a red, white and blue bikini top that Hailey was pretty sure had been made for a woman half her cup size. A black cowboy hat covered her bleached-blond hair and calf-hugging patent-leather biker boots completed the look. Kid couldn't seem to tear his eyes away.

Hailey rose from her crouched position on the ground and wadded up the blue buff cloth. Years of playing catch with her brother had given her a decent arm. She aimed straight for the smirk on Kid's face. She nailed it. For a second, she wasn't sure who looked more surprised Kid, or the woman, but then she reminded herself that she didn't care.

"I'm going for a walk," she said. Kid opened his mouth to say something, but Hailey snapped, "And don't try to stop me."

The woman looked from her to Kid with her eyebrows raised, but Hailey just spun on her heel and walked away. She'd had enough of Kid and his bossy attitude. It wasn't as if she were his paid employee. She was happy to help out, but he couldn't tell her what to do or how to behave. It wasn't as if he could fire her. Besides, the way he'd been drooling over the blond bimbo with the huge ta-tas, he'd probably forgotten that she'd even come with them.

Hailey circled their booth and stopped short. The place had filled to capacity while she'd been busy scraping smashed bug guts off headlights. Leather vests, tattoos and skimpy tops flooded her vision. Wow. She stepped back into the shadow of the tent. She needed to get her bearings.

She looked down at the triple-XL shirt hanging down to her knees and she felt like someone's babushka. Madeline wouldn't be caught dead in this shirt, and neither would she.

She pulled the shirt over her head and stuffed it under the blue plastic sheet that comprised the side wall of their booth. Kid had not specifically stated that she must wear it at all times. She would put it back on when she was in the booth. Otherwise, she was just another visitor at the rally. She adjusted her halter top to give herself maximum lift. She glanced down at her jeans and frowned. None of the other women were wearing this much. How to fix this? She wondered.

She'd seen a pair of scissors in the van. She hurried around the back of the booth to where Chooch had parked it. Kid was still chatting with the blonde, but he kept glancing over her hat as if looking for something or someone. Maybe the judges were coming.

Hailey shucked her jeans and grabbed the scissors. She cut them as high as she dared to go. When she slid them back on, she felt a cool draft up the back. It was exciting in a slutty sort of way. She topped off the look with her butt-stomping black boots and tied her hair back with a black bandanna. She climbed out of the van and checked her reflection in the overlarge side mirror...she looked like a badass biker girl. Hell, yeah! Hailey stifled her laugh with her hand. She grabbed the box of postcards for The Chop Shop that she had stashed in the van, because she was going to litter the rally with ads. Kid could be dealt with later.

SHE'D BEEN GONE FOR AN HOUR. A walk didn't take an hour. A walk that led to trouble took no more than thirty minutes. Kid frowned. The judges were going from booth to booth. They'd be here in minutes. They expected him to be here, as well, but he couldn't stand not knowing where Hailey was. She was his responsibility and he couldn't let anything happen to her.

"Uncle Pete," he said, "I'm going for a walk."

"But the judges…" Pete protested, his face wrinkling up and then creasing with a grin. "What's the matter? Afraid she's having fun?"

"No, I'm sure she's locked herself in a Porta Potty somewhere, scared to death."

"This is going to be my sweetest win yet," Uncle Pete said. "Go find your girl. I'll finesse the judges."

"She's not my girl," Kid said.

"You want to bet?" Pete asked with a laugh.

Kid frowned. "Just tell the judges what they need to know," he said and stomped away.

She wasn't his girl. She was a huge pain in his ass, but she surely wasn't his girl. Her type enjoyed a good tumble with a bad boy, but it was the Boy Scouts that they wanted to bankroll them for the rest of their lives.

He walked all of the booths. He searched high and low for a medium-height, medium-build brunette wearing a huge black T-shirt. He never found her. He did find a bombshell wearing a red halter top and risqué cutoffs sitting astride a purple chopper with silver flames while she sucked down a margarita the size of a fishbowl. Standing beside her was his main competitor and rival on the East Coast, Jimbo "the Jackass" Jackson of J-Squared Choppers. Okay, so he added the jackass part.

"Jimbo," Kid greeted the portly, middle-aged man with the gray mullet and large yellow sunglasses. "How are you?"

"Jim-dandy," the jackass replied with a grin. "I caught me a regular belle of the ball, don't you think?"

Kid glowered at Hailey. She gave him a wobbly smile and a finger wave.

"Hey, there."

"Peaches, how many margaritas have you had?" he asked.

Hailey frowned while considering his question. She tipped forward a little when she answered, "I don't believe I kept count."

"You know her?" Jimbo asked.

"Oh, yeah," Kid said, refusing to explain about the auction or that she worked for him. "I'm sort of babysitting her today."

"More like *babe*sitting," Jimbo said with a guffaw. "I'll be happy to take her off your hands."

"Thanks, but…" Kid caught Hailey as she wobbled backward, nearly slipping off of the chopper. He righted her and turned to Jimbo and said, "She looks smashed."

"That's just the way I like 'em," Jimbo said with a leer. "They're less inhibited that way."

Kid resisted the urge to put a fist in his face. Barely. Jimbo appeared to have invested quite a bit of tequila in Hailey. He knew Jimbo wouldn't let her go without an argument. Kid sighed. He figured he could force his way out of here and end up in a fight or he could show the jackass the bigger picture.

"Peaches, what usually happens when you drink too much?" he asked.

"I throw up," she said with an unladylike hiccup. "Then I drink some more."

"That a girl!" Jimbo pumped his fist.

"How are you feeling right now?" Kid asked.

"Not so good." Hailey met his gaze and winked. Kid frowned. For a split second, she didn't look drunk at all. "I think I'm going to be sick."

"Hey, is that one of the choppers you're having judged?" Kid asked Jimbo. "I don't think they give trophies for hurl."

Hailey made a deep retching sound and Jimbo leaped to her side. "Not on the bike. Not on the bike!" He grabbed

Hailey about the waist and hauled her off the bike and thrust her at Kid.

"Get her out of here, man. I can't have my area stinking of puke."

"Sure," Kid said. "I'll take care of her."

Kid carried Hailey past Jimbo's booth. When they were out of sight, he set her down none too gently.

"I can't believe you're drunk," he said. "As if there isn't enough to do, now I have to take care of you."

"Get real," Hailey said and pushed away from him. She began to saunter between the booths, leaving Kid no choice but to follow.

"I went to college," she said. "I can hold my alcohol."

She stumbled and caught herself on the corner of a leather biker-wear booth.

"Okay, I'm a little tipsy because I missed lunch, but I'm not drunk," she said. "But I am hungry."

She began to walk again, scanning the booths for food.

"Then what was that about?" he asked, still following.

"Nothing much," she said with a shrug. "I was walking around asking questions and I remembered that he's your biggest competition, so I thought I'd ask him about his choppers. Ugh!"

"And then what happened?" Kid asked, hanging on to his patience with a tenuous grasp.

"Well, he trashed you and The Chop Shop. He said you were cut-rate and a no-talent. Then he shoved a margarita in my hand and tossed me onto one of his choppers. He kept filling up my glass, so I figured the only way I was going to get out of there was to pretend to pass out and have someone call a paramedic. Of course, he may figure it out when he goes to fire up the chopper."

"Figure what out?" he asked.

"That I was pouring the margaritas into the gas tank," she said.

"You didn't." Kid doubled up with laughter. "Peaches, you are something else."

"I bet Jimbo has another name for me," she said. "What an ass."

"You know, if you'd left your T-shirt on, this never would have happened," he said. "By the way, what happened to your jeans?"

"They had an unfortunate incident with a pair of scissors," she said. "The T-shirt was a muumuu. I'd have had heatstroke if I'd kept it on."

Kid wanted to be pissed at her, but she looked so damned good, he was too distracted to stay angry. Instead, he was charmed. It was very annoying. "Let's get back to the booth."

"I'll meet you there," Hailey said. "I need food or I really will pass out."

"Oh, no," Kid said with a shake of the head. "I'll go with you. The last thing I need is for you to get swept into an impromptu mud-wrestling contest or, even worse, a wet T-shirt contest."

"Why not?" Hailey asked. "Don't you think I could win?"

"I refuse to discuss this on the grounds that I might incriminate myself," he said.

"Interesting," she said, but she didn't push it.

Kid almost sighed with relief.

"I'll be quick," she promised. "First booth I see, I'll grab something."

The fourth booth they passed had the barbecue.

"I don't suppose they have barbecue tofu?" she asked.

"'Fraid not," he said.

"Fine. I'll have a half rack of ribs and some hot links," she ordered at the window.

"Beans or potato salad?" asked the sweaty, red-faced man taking the order.

"Beans, and a beer to wash it all down," she said.

"Make it two of everything and a bag of peanuts," Kid said, stepping up behind her. Before Hailey could pull the money out of her pocket, Kid handed the man a twenty.

"I'm hungry, too," he said.

"Let's hurry back to the booth," she said as they grabbed their trays of food. "We don't want to miss the judges."

"I'm sure we already did."

"Oh, sorry," she said. She dunked a slice of Wonder bread into the extra sauce and bit into it. "Hey, this isn't half-bad. It's no alfalfa-sprout muffin…"

"Amen," he said. She gave him a baleful stare, which he ignored.

"Come on, let's get out of the crowd," he said.

Kid found a clear spot underneath the shade of an old, gnarled maple. He knew he should be hustling back to the booth, but he found himself reluctant to let go of this time with Hailey. Every time he thought he had her pegged, she surprised him. He found himself wanting to know what made her tick.

She bit into a rib and a smear of sauce coated her cheek. Kid smiled. With so much leg showing and not a little cleavage, she looked like a biker chick. Too bad she wasn't. The urge to let his hands slide up those legs… Kid coughed on a bite of barbecue. He could not be having thoughts like that of her. He'd never get through the rest of the month at that rate.

Hailey wasn't his type. He watched as she wiped the sauce off her cheek with the back of her hand. Or was she? There was something so very grounded about Hailey that made Kid wonder if he was right about her after all. Then he saw the enticing V made by her cleavage and he wondered if it was just his penis shouting louder than his common sense.

"Tell me about your life," he said. That should do it. A few stories about nannies and boarding school and his libido would be under control again.

"What?" she asked.

"Tell me something about Hailey Fitzwilly," he said.

"Is that the beer talking?" she asked. "Or do you really want to know?"

"I want to know," he said. "I find you...interesting."

Hailey snorted. Kid lifted his brows in surprise.

"I'm not interesting," she said. "I'm a workaholic who is prone to ulcers and I'm frequently nervous, but I'm not interesting."

"Why are you nervous?" he asked, studying her.

"I'm afraid of disappointing people. More specifically, I'm afraid of disappointing my mother."

"In what way?" he asked.

"In every way," she said. "I try very hard to live up to her expectations, but I have crashed and burned a lot lately."

"I can't imagine that," he said with a shake of his head. "It seems to me like you can do anything you choose. Frankly, I never know what to expect from you. Just when I think I've figured you out, you surprise me."

Hailey laughed and Kid tried to look offended. She laughed even harder. He was glad. He had been trying to make her smile. It bothered him that she felt like a failure. He couldn't imagine anything further from the truth. Hell, she had sold five choppers and wrangled him into building one for charity, hadn't she?

"What about you?" she asked. "What makes Kid Cassidy tick?"

"I'm very simple," he said. "I like my machines fast, my women hot and my beer cold."

"That's it?" she asked.

"Pretty much," he said.

"I don't think so," she said with a shake of her head. She finished her ribs and wadded up the wrapper. A trash can was ten feet away. She tossed the wrapper but it bounced off the rim and rolled back toward her.

Kid watched silently as she rose and bent to retrieve it. This morning, she'd been in an innocent pair of jeans. There was nothing innocent about her newly shorn shorts. The woman had the sweetest pair of legs. He had to bite his cheek and turn away before he did something stupid, such as wolf whistle or howl.

"What do you mean you don't think so?" he asked, finishing his ribs and tossing the wrapper into the trash can. Nothing but net. She gave him an annoyed look.

"You're full of it," she said. "And I don't mean barbecue."

He rose to stand beside her. The top of her head reached his nose. She was a good height for pulling close and… Kid shook his head. He wasn't going there.

"You take care of Uncle Pete, Chooch and Mikey," she said. "You're trying to mediate the situation between Stan and Irene, even though you have nothing to gain from it and neither of them is being particularly helpful. Your business is successful despite the small setback you're facing."

"Oh, really?" he asked. "You think having my business manager run off is a small setback?"

"Absolutely," she said. "You're going to be huge. Trust me. I know these things."

"Hey, Kid," a man wearing a muscle shirt shouted as he passed them. "Nice flyer, stud boy."

The man tossed a postcard at them and Kid caught it.

One side listed information about the shop and the car dealership that would now be selling Kid's choppers. The other side was the photo of Kid astride a cherry-red chopper.

"Where did this come from?" he asked.

He glanced up to see Hailey sprinting into the crowd. He grabbed her by the back of the shorts and pulled her back. Then he held the card in front of her nose.

"Explain," he said.

"It's sort of like a business card," she said. "I had them made up for our mailing list."

"We have a mailing list?"

"We will," she said. "And I thought the rally would be a good place to hand out a few."

"How many?" he asked.

"Five... hundred," she said. "They've been very popular, especially with the ladies."

"Why did I ever let you out of my sight?" he asked and smacked his forehead with his hand. "You would think I would know better by now. I am going to look like a narcissistic jerk."

"No, you're going to be a huge success," she said. Then she hit him with her velvet-brown eyes and said, "Trust me."

Her do-rag was cockeyed. Kid tried to resist the urge to fix it. He failed. Her sweet-smelling, soft-brown curls wrapped themselves about his hands while he straightened the black bandanna on her head.

He felt her breath hitch when his fingers brushed the warm skin at the nape of her neck. So, she felt it, too. Somehow this didn't make Kid feel any better.

"We'd better get back," he said, not sure whether he wanted to strangle her or kiss her. "Uncle Pete is probably wondering where we are."

Hailey cleared her throat and nodded. As they passed

through the throngs of people that clogged the rally, Kid kept one hand at Hailey's back. He wasn't letting her out of his sight again.

THE CHOP SHOP SCORED THREE large trophies and several ribbons. Kid was pleased. More importantly, they'd taken seven more orders for choppers, making their wait list close to a year long. He didn't want to know whether the flyers or the trophies were responsible, but he couldn't deny the fact that they had never gotten that many orders at a one-day rally before.

He'd had to turn down one pushy celebrity. Just because the guy sang in a hip hop band, he thought he should get moved to the front of the list. Uh, no. Kid would rather build a chopper for a regular guy who busted his butt to earn the bread for it than some candyass hip-hop star who had more money than sense and just wanted another toy. He was very democratic that way.

Hailey had seemed impressed with his evenhandedness, despite the loss of the celebrity as free advertising. Kid tried not to dwell on it. It wasn't as if he cared what she thought....

He glanced at the van's passenger seat. She was sound asleep. He wasn't sure what had possessed him to tell Chooch to drive the winning chopper home while he took the van. Oh, fine, he knew what had possessed him. Hailey. She was sucking him in like a whirlpool and he didn't have the strength to swim against the current.

He didn't want to like her this much. He had to remember that her presence was only for a charitable cause and that was it. Once the chopper was built and the auction over, he'd never see her again.

He stopped at a red light and glanced at her. She looked cold. He grabbed the overlarge T-shirt from where it lay on the floor of the van and tucked it around her shoulders. She burrowed into it. Kid slid his hand down her arm and his fingers accidentally brushed the side of her breast. He jerked back. Great, she was asleep and he was copping a feel. Now he could add *dirtbag* to his list of undesirable traits.

"Something wrong?" Her voice was raspy with sleep.

Kid turned and met her gaze. It hit him then. This was the sort of woman that made a man wreck his life. She was funny, gorgeous and smart. And if he fell under her spell, the next thing he knew he'd be having his tattoos removed, selling the shop, putting on a suit and pimping insurance. Heaven help him.

"Nothing's wrong. But I think you might be better off at another chopper shop."

6

"WHAT?" HAILEY SAT BOLT UPRIGHT. "You're bailing on me?"

Kid looked away from her as if trying to avoid the shocked hurt in her eyes.

"I'm not bailing," he said. "Not exactly."

He turned into the parking lot of The Chop Shop and parked the van. He climbed out of the van, his back straight and his jaw set as if bracing himself for the argument ahead.

The lights were on and the winning choppers had been parked in the garage and locked up for the night. The rest of the guys must have gone home already. Good, Hailey thought. She didn't want anyone trying to referee this shouting match.

"Not bailing?" She popped open her door and hopped out. The night air was chilly and she yanked the T-shirt over her head with furious tugs. "What do you call it, then? We had a deal and you're backing out."

"No, I'll still donate all of the parts, but I think maybe you'd do better with someone else building it."

"Like who?" Hailey snapped. "Jimbo? Terrific. I'll probably have to sleep with him just to get the tires put on. Heaven knows what he'll expect for a paint job."

"No! Not him," Kid protested. "But somebody."

"Why?" she asked. "What made you change your mind?"

"Nothing," he said, looking evasive. "We just got these new orders, and I've got the whole Stan-and-Irene debacle happening."

It sounded lame. Something was bothering Kid, but he wasn't going to tell her what. She didn't have time for this. If Kid wanted out, so be it.

"Fine," she said. "I'll find someone else."

Hailey stomped away from him and into the break room. She wasn't going to cry. It would ruin her mascara and make her look like a sissy. Besides, just because she'd spent a week and a half trying to get the dolt to help her and now he was bailing was no reason to cry. She hiccupped. It hurt. Still, she wouldn't give in.

"Are you going to be okay?" he asked, following her into the break room.

"What do you care?" she asked. She opened her locker, on which one of the guys had scrawled *Peaches* in grease, and pulled out her favorite gray hoodie. She jerked it on. Her legs were cold and she wished she hadn't trashed a perfectly good pair of jeans just so she could fit into Kid Cassidy's world. What had she been thinking? Everything had seemed to go so well, but here he was giving her the boot.

"Hailey, I care," he said.

"Yeah, sure," she snorted. "It's not me you're letting down, you know. It's the hundreds of sick kids who would benefit from this auction by receiving better equipment and more staff."

"I said I'd still supply the parts," he said.

"Yeah, but who is going to build the bike? It has to be finished in two weeks," she said.

She turned to stare at him. He didn't meet her gaze. So, he felt badly about this. Good. But still she didn't understand.

"Why did you change your mind?" she asked. She wanted to know. There had to be a reason.

"Because I'm an idiot," he said looking chagrined. He gave her a wry smile and a shrug. "I guess I was just feeling overwhelmed by the amount of orders we have right now. You're right. I promised to build it and I will."

"You mean it?" she asked. "Really?"

"Yes," he said. He looked as happy about it as he would about a root canal.

"Oh, thank you," she said.

She threw her arms about his neck and hugged him close. She felt him stiffen beneath her grasp but she was too relieved to care. She wasn't totally screwed.

She stepped back from him and grinned. Relief must have been shining from her like a beacon because he actually blinked as if the glare was too much. She was so relieved, and not just because he was still going to help her pull this off but because she couldn't imagine not seeing him every day. The realization hit her right between the eyes like a dart. She had a crush on Kid Cassidy.

"Wow," she said.

"Wow what?" he asked, his goatee framing his smile in the most becoming way. Hailey felt herself get hot from the inside out. Uh-oh.

"I was just thinking," she said, scanning the garage to find something, anything, to distract her from her new reality. "I was thinking I should learn how to ride a chopper."

"You?" Kid laughed. Hailey felt her warm feelings toward him freeze over like a sudden ice age.

"What's so funny?" she asked.

"You on a chopper," he said. He turned back and headed toward the garage. "How long has it been since you've been on a regular bike?"

"A year or four," she said. "So?"

"You're a cream puff. You could never hold your own on a chopper," he teased.

He hauled a large cardboard box from the back of the van and began to unpack it. It was full of sample parts that he had picked up at the rally.

"Oh, yeah?" she asked, feeling goaded by his doubt. "There's a lot you don't know about me. I'll have you know I studied kickboxing."

Kid rolled his eyes and made to walk around her toward the supply shelves. Hailey neatly kicked the tailpipe out of his hands and it skidded across the floor with a clatter. It was very impressive—and the only move she knew.

Kid turned to face her with his hands on his hips.

"You're going to buff those scratches out," he said.

Hailey shrugged. "What's the matter? Afraid you can't take me?"

She started bobbing and weaving around him, kicking and punching the air for all she was worth.

"You're not seriously challenging me are you?" he asked.

She tapped him in the back of the knee with the toe of her boot. His leg wobbled but didn't buckle.

He shook his head at her. "You're making a mistake."

"I'm no cream puff," she said and faked a jab at his ribs.

Kid grabbed her about the knees and took her to the floor in one sweep. He cradled her head and her back with his arms, but she still landed on the concrete with an *oomph* as her dignity left her on a rush of air.

What had started as a joke was no longer funny. There was no denying the concrete at her back or the weight of the man lying atop her. She wrapped her arms about his neck. He strained away from her as if he knew what she was about to do, but he didn't let go.

She twined her arms tighter about his neck and pulled herself up against him. He resisted. His lips were clamped shut. He was fighting her for all he was worth. Still, Hailey couldn't stop herself. She placed her lips upon his.

It was a firm, dry kiss. They might as well have been siblings. It wasn't enough, not nearly enough. She wrapped her leg about his waist and used all of her weight to leverage him back on top of her. Then she kissed him again. It was still dry, but his mouth began to soften.

She felt his shoulders tighten as if he would break out of this embrace if he could. She couldn't let him go. She had to know. She placed her mouth on his again. As if against his will, his mouth sealed onto hers. Together, their lips parted just slightly and the hot warmth of their tongues met in an intimate greeting that left Hailey feeling rocked from the inside out.

"Kid Cassidy, I know you're in there," Irene shouted through one of the bay doors. "Don't try to hide from me again."

"No," Kid said as he rolled off Hailey. "Not today. I was having such a good day."

He hauled her up to her feet and Hailey watched as he strode over to the side door. He yanked it open and pulled the woman in the fuzzy pink bathrobe into the garage. She was clutching a half-eaten lemon meringue pie.

"Hailey, this is Irene. Irene, this is Hailey," he introduced them. "Irene, I've left five messages a day for Stan on his voice mail since the day he left. He's not answering. I don't know what to tell you."

Hailey looked at the petite, dark-haired woman with pity. She looked so sad and lost and covered in meringue.

"So, what are you, the new flavor of the month?" Irene snapped at her and Hailey frowned. She no longer felt sorry for her.

She shook her head and wagged a finger between her and Kid. "Us? Oh, no, I just work here."

"Yeah, so did that husband-stealing slut, Marie," Irene growled.

"Do not take your temper out on Hailey," Kid said. "She's actually doing Stan's job in return for the donation of a chopper for the Children's Hospital auction. She's been keeping us in the black. She's sold more than a dozen choppers in a week and a half. If this keeps up, I'll have to hire more staff and expand."

Irene shoved a bite of pie into her mouth. "I'm sorry. I'm not myself."

"It's all right," Hailey assured her. "No hard feelings."

"I need him back," Irene said and then broke into huge, elephantine sobs.

Hailey and Kid exchanged an alarmed look. Kid gestured for her to do something. Hailey shook her head. He sighed and wrapped an awkward arm around Irene.

"He'll be back," he said. "Hey, the way Hailey is outselling him, he'd better come back soon or I won't take him back."

Kid froze as if a sudden thought had just struck him.

"Hold her," he said and shoved the still-sobbing Irene into Hailey's arms and disappeared into his office.

"There, there," Hailey said as she patted the woman's back and tried to ignore the smear of pie on her favorite hoodie.

He reappeared looking quite pleased with himself. Hailey shoved Irene and her pie back into his arms.

"See you on Monday. And I am going to learn how to ride a chopper," she said.

He looked at her over Irene's head. One eyebrow was raised higher than the other. It just made her more determined.

"Tomorrow is Sunday," he said. "Why don't you take a day off to do some yoga and find yourself again. In the light of a new day, I'm sure your interest in learning to ride will be gone."

"We'll see, won't we?" she asked. She strolled out of the garage to her car without saying another word.

So, THE BALANCE THING TOOK a little practice, but otherwise she felt as if she was doing pretty well zipping down the road at a reasonable twenty-five miles per hour. Okay, three drivers had honked at her and one had shot her the bird, but it wasn't her fault. They were road hogs.

At the stop sign, Hailey glanced at her watch. She was late—again. Oh, well. When Kid saw her zoom into the lot, he'd be so surprised he'd forget that she was late. She hoped.

Hailey hopped up onto the curb. All of the garage doors were open, and she could see the guys were already suited up in their coveralls. At the sight of her, all work ceased. She saw a grin crease Uncle Pete's face, and she made a loop around the parking lot just to show off.

She switched off the engine and pulled off her helmet. She was just tossing her hair back over her shoulder when Kid appeared in the doorway. His mouth hung open as if the hinge was broken.

"What the hell is that?" he asked.

She thought she heard someone snort. She looked at the guys and they all quickly glanced up, as if the rafters in the garage had suddenly become infinitely fascinating.

Hailey slid off the seat and set the kickstand. "It's a Vespa."

"A *whata?*" Kid asked.

"It's a scooter," she said.

"Uh-huh," he said, walking over to look at it.

His black hair was still damp from his morning shower and he was wearing the coveralls that had the sleeves ripped off. Hailey tried not to think about his kiss. She failed and grew warm all over.

"Do you like it?" she asked. "Pretty snappy, huh?"

"Snappy," he repeated as he examined the bright-pink scooter with the Scooby-Doo flowers all over it. "What's in the engine? Hamsters?"

"I'll have you know that it can go more than thirty-five miles per hour," she said.

"A whole thirty-five?" Mikey asked as he joined them. "Wow. I would have thought the hamsters would pull their little hamstrings at ten miles per hour."

"Maybe they eat a lot of cheese—you know, to make gas for an alternative fuel," Uncle Pete said and punched Mikey on the arm. They dissolved into laughter.

"Very funny," Hailey snapped. "I'll have you know that these are very popular in Europe."

"Hey, Chooch," Mikey called, still laughing. "Come look. I don't think you could fit your big toe on here."

Chooch strolled out of the garage, still grinning.

"Where did you get that thing?" he asked Hailey.

"I borrowed it from my friend Madeline. You remember her," Hailey said. "The pretty woman with the long, dark hair and the terrific figure?" At their chorus of nods, she continued, "It's hers. She likes to ride it around the neighborhood—naked."

It was an outrageous lie, but she knew Madeline wouldn't mind. And it sure wiped the smirks off their faces. Except for Kid, who laughed.

Miffed, Hailey plopped her matching pink helmet onto the seat. "I don't see what is so funny. I want to learn how to ride a chopper and I thought this was a good starting place."

"I'll teach you how to ride a chopper," Mikey volunteered.

"You will?" she asked.

"No," Kid said. "My insurance won't cover that accident waiting to happen."

"I won't teach her here," Mikey said. "I'll take her down to the old drive-in theater—you know, where you took me. It's overgrown, so if she wipes out, it'll be okay."

"No," Kid said. "I don't want her learning any of your bad habits. If anyone is going to teach her, it'll be me."

"Yeah!" Hailey began to jump for joy, but Kid's dark look made her rethink it and she just rocked up on her heels instead.

"Okay, that's enough," Kid said, ending the conversation. "Park this thing in back. I don't want people to see it in front of my garage. It's embarrassing."

"It is not embarrassing," she protested.

Kid picked up her helmet and plopped it onto her head. "Yes, it is. In engine terms, it's like having a Wee Willy Winkie hanging out of my pants. Park it in back."

Hailey felt her cheeks grow hot. Wee willy winkie, her foot! She'd seen his and it… She shook her head. Again, it was probably best not to go there.

After she locked the Vespa up in back, she found Kid in the break room studying her notes from the rally. A drawing pad was next to him and he was making sketches off her notes.

"Does this look like what you were thinking?" he asked.

She glanced over his shoulder. It was a terrific sketch. He obviously had some artistic training, or at least a real knack for it.

"That's exactly it," she said. "A soft-tail frame with a twisted springer fork."

Kid looked at her and frowned. "Do you even know what that means?"

"Soft tail means it won't break your butt, according to Uncle Pete, and a springer fork is the cool, twisty metal thingy that goes down to the front wheel," Hailey said.

Kid grunted.

"How's Irene?" she asked.

"She's okay. She promised to shower today, and I have high hopes that Stan is going to reappear very soon. So, are you ready?"

"Ready?" she asked.

"We're going parts-shopping today."

"Shopping?"

"For your parts," he said. "I have a soft-tail frame here that we can use. That's the foundation of the chopper. Everything else is an accessory."

"You mean it?" she asked. "We're going to start today."

"We'll get the parts today," he said. "Tomorrow we'll make the mock-up."

Hailey could feel another bounce of excitement coming on. She tried to contain it and just rocked up on her toes instead.

Kid grinned at her. "Go," he said. "I'll meet you in the van in five."

Hailey was so excited, she ran to the van. She didn't want Kid to change his mind.

They were cruising down I-95 when Hailey saw it looming up ahead. Oh, crap! She didn't think it would have been put up so fast. Still, he looked magnificent. But somehow she had a feeling he wouldn't think so.

"Hey, Kid, look over there. Is that one of your choppers?" she asked and pointed out the window at nothing.

Kid looked. "Where?" he asked.

"Over there," she said. "On the other side of that minivan."

He strained to see. Then he glanced back at the road and his eyes drifted to the left. He hit the brakes. With a sharp turn and some burnt rubber, Kid hauled the van over two lanes and braked hard.

He stared up at his own image, larger than life, looming over eight lanes of traffic. His jaw was slack. He blinked a few times. Then his head slowly swiveled in her direction.

"Or I could have been referring to that chopper up there," she said. She smiled but he didn't smile in return.

"I'm going to have to leave the state," he said. "Maybe even the country. The rest of the biker community is going to think I am the biggest ass on the planet."

"No," she said. "The sad truth, Kid Cassidy, is that you have 'it'. Women are going to want you and men are going to want to be you."

"Do me a favor," Kid said as he started up the engine. "Don't talk. Just don't talk."

"Okay, I just—" she began, but he interrupted. "Not a word."

Hailey sat back in her seat with her lips pressed tightly together. Well, at least he hadn't booted her out of the van. She glanced up at the billboard as they passed. Kid could whine all he wanted, but he was hot and the billboard was hot and he was going to be huge. She could feel that old, wonderful zing pulsing through her when she looked at the billboard. Kid was going to be a huge success, and for the first time in a long time, she savored the feeling of a successful campaign.

FIVE HOURS LATER, HAILEY FELT as if her brain had congealed into tapioca. The van was full of parts. The sheer enormity of the task ahead left her feeling queasy. How was Kid going to assemble this chopper and have it ready in two weeks?

"You okay?" Kid asked as they zipped south on I-95 back toward Fairfield. He reached into the box of French fries that sat in the drink holder between them and grabbed a bunch.

"Yes…no." Hailey glanced over her shoulder at the boxes of parts. "Is this going to be ready on time?"

"Don't flake out on me now," he said. "We just invested thousands of dollars in parts."

"I'm not flaking out. I'm freaking out. It was one thing to quit my advertising job in Manhattan to open a yoga studio in Westport. At least I know yoga, and I'm an okay teacher. It's sort of boring, but not stressful. And that's what I wanted, no more stress. So, what I am doing now? Making myself insane by working against the clock for a charity auction. I don't know a caliper from a clutch. How do we know this chopper is going to be a success?"

"So, you were in advertising," he said. "Well, that explains it."

"Explains what?" she asked.

"The billboard. The flyers," he said. "You're all about packaging and marketing. I bet you were good."

"Uh." Hailey refused to comment. She did not want Kid to know that she had crashed and burned or that her claim to fame was an adult-diaper jingle. It was so uncool.

"Peaches, you're spiraling on me," he said. "There's no need to panic. It's going to be fine. Try thinking about the paint job instead."

"Paint job?" she asked. "What paint job?"

"What design are you going to put on it?" he asked. "You saw the choppers at the rally. What are you planning for the charity chopper?"

"Planning?" she asked with a note of hysteria in her voice. "I don't know. Blue is a nice color."

"Yeah, blue is nice," he agreed.

"Oh, man," Hailey moaned and put her head in her hands. "This chopper is going to suck. I'll be lucky if anyone bids on it."

"You're panicking again," Kid said. "Think of something that inspires you and see if you can translate that into paint."

"Is that what you do?" she asked and he nodded. She stared at the road ahead of them, willing an idea to spring forth. Then it hit her.

"Kid, get off at this exit," she said. "Hurry. Now!"

"Why?" he asked as he cut across a lane and turned down the ramp.

"I just thought of what inspires me," she said.

He followed her directions all the way to the Children's Hospital. They parked in the visitors' section and Hailey was out of the van and striding toward the doors. She knew just who to ask for help.

KID FOLLOWED. SHE LOOKED LIKE a woman on a mission, which was much better than the sickly girl who had been sitting beside him a few minutes ago. He supposed he could have eased her mind and let her know that he fully intended to make sure this chopper was built to his usual high standards, but since she'd been driving him crazy for two weeks now, he didn't think it would hurt to let her suffer a little bit of doubt.

"Hi, Amy," Hailey greeted a woman in scrubs behind a large counter.

"Hail, it's good to see you," the petite Asian woman said, grinning. "It's not your usual day, is it?"

"No, I'm just popping in to see some of the children," she said.

"They're in the playroom," Amy said.

"Oh, perfect. This is Kid. He's with me."

"Hi." Kid waved at the woman. Her eyes went round with surprise, but she recovered with a quick smile. "Hi."

Hailey led Kid down a brightly colored hallway covered in artwork. Children's renderings of their families and pets and a rainbow of other images greeted him. For a hospital, it certainly had a positive and happy feel about it.

They wound around a corner to a large, brightly decorated room. Children of all ages were playing in groups. Toddlers wrestled with brightly colored foam blocks in one corner while some older children had a puppet show going. Hailey opened the door and slid inside. Kid followed her.

A chorus of yells greeted them as several of the children recognized Hailey. They mobbed her as if she were a rock star. Hailey dispensed hugs and kisses like a pro. No child was missed. Kid felt something tight squeeze his chest as he watched. She was amazing.

"Hailey," a stout woman with tight gray curls and a wide smile shouted above the children's howls. "So nice to see you. Are you here to pull an extra shift?"

"Hi, Sophie. Actually, I need some help and I think the children might just have my answer."

The woman raised her brows in interest. "How can they help?"

"Miss Hailey, Miss Hailey, do you like my dress?" a little girl no more than four pirouetted in front of Hailey in a costume that looked as if it was inspired by Disney.

"I do, Brianna," Hailey said. "Why, you look just like Belle."

The little girl beamed and danced away in a flurry of circles.

"I need inspiration," Hailey said to Sophie. She gestured behind her. "Kid and I are building a chopper for the hospital auction, but I have no idea what to paint on it."

"Well, you came to the right place," Sophie said as she grabbed a boy running past her. She hugged him close and whispered, "Walk" in his ear before she released him. He scampered off with a nod. "These kids are nothing if not inspirational."

"Miss Sophie," one of the toddlers wailed from across the room.

"Excuse me," she said. "Duty calls."

"Come on, I'll introduce you around," Hailey said and she dragged Kid toward a red and yellow, kid-size table covered in Play-Doh and paint.

"Hi Matty, Luke, Jamie and Sarah," she said as she squatted beside their table. "What are you guys working on?"

"We're painting," Matty answered.

"This is my friend Kid," Hailey said as he crouched down beside her. "Guess what he does?"

"Is he your boyfriend?" Sarah asked.

"No, just a friend," Hailey said quickly, but Kid noticed that she was blushing.

Sarah sidled closer to Kid. "Hi," she said and batted her eyelashes at him.

Hailey's lips twitched as if she was trying not to laugh.

"I think he's a fireman," Luke said as he pushed his glasses up on his nose to study Kid.

Kid noticed that the boy had no hair under his ball cap and he wondered if he'd lost it due to chemo treatments. He forced a note of cheer into his voice. "Nope, I don't fight fires."

"I think he's a superhero like the X-Men," Matty said. "Look at his arms. I bet he could rip the doors off cars with muscles like that."

"A superhero?" Kid repeated. "I like that, but no, I can't jump over tall buildings in a single bound."

"Can you melt things with your eyes?" the third little boy, Jamie, asked. He was thin and pale and looked as if a stiff breeze would knock him over.

"Nope," Kid answered. He felt Hailey watching him so he turned to face her. "Although, it would certainly come in handy sometimes."

He glanced at her top and saw her face blush an even

deeper shade of pink. He supposed he shouldn't tease her since he was the one who had been resistant last night. But the truth was, he hadn't been able to get her kiss or her scent or *her* out of his mind ever since.

"He builds choppers," Hailey said, clearing her throat. "And we're going to build one for the hospital auction and make money with it."

"Sweet," Matty said.

"So what I need from you is some ideas of how we should paint it," she said.

"I like pink and purple," Sarah said.

"Eww," Luke snorted. "No way. It'd be a total sissy bike."

"How about a wizard?" Jamie asked. "Like from *Harry Potter*."

Hailey looked at Kid. "Is that possible?"

"Anything is possible if we make the tank big enough," he said.

"No, no wizards," Luke said. "Make it a superhero, with webbing and junk. That would be cool."

"Can you believe that's already been done?" Kid asked. "One of the coolest choppers I've ever seen. Even the wheels had webs."

"I have an idea," Matty said. He rose from the table and walked over toward a supply shelf. Kid noticed that his pant leg looked thin and that his gait was uneven. A prosthetic leg.

"Hey, how's the new peg?" Hailey asked.

"It's okay, but I get tired," Matty said with a shrug.

"Have you run on it yet?" she asked.

"About fifty feet," he said with a note of pride in his voice. "And I didn't fall—not once."

"Stupendous!" Hailey said with genuine awe in her voice, and she high-fived him.

Kid felt the same way about her right now.

Matty came back to the table with a bright yellow sheet of paper. He laid it down and then stuck his hand in a tub of blue paint. Very neatly, he made a perfect blue handprint.

He looked at Hailey and asked, "What do you think? Maybe we could cover the whole bike with our hand-prints and then it really would be from all of us?"

"Is this possible?" Hailey asked Kid.

"Sure," Kid said. "If we bring him this sheet of paper, our paint guy can reproduce their artwork on the bike. I think we need more handprints, though."

"Cool. Matty, you're a genius!" Hailey cried and gave him a big, smacking kiss on the head. Matty turned bright red and Jamie nudged him and teased, "Matty likes Hai-ley."

"Watch it or I'll kiss you, too," Hailey said and made big smacking noises with her mouth. Jamie crawled under the table and all of the kids cracked up.

"Let's get everyone to help," Sarah suggested.

In short order, Kid and Hailey had several sheets of yellow paper covered in red, blue and green handprints of all different sizes.

As the kids were ushered out of the playroom, they waved exuberant goodbyes to Hailey and Kid.

"Will we get to see the chopper when it's finished?" Jamie asked as he lingered by the door.

"I promise I'll drive it over as soon as it's done," Kid said.

"Sweet," Matty said. "I can't wait to tell my dad."

"Thanks, Sophie," Hailey called from the door. "I'll see you on Friday."

Sophie waved from where she was helping Brianna re-luctantly take off her princess costume.

"How do you do this every week?" Kid asked as they exited the building and headed toward the van.

"It's easy," Hailey said. "They're great kids."

"But some of them…" Kid hesitated. "Isn't it hard?"

"Sometimes," Hailey said. "But it'd be harder not to be here to help or be a part of their lives."

Kid took the papers that she held and gently laid them on top of the parts in the back of the van. A small red handprint the size of his thumb caught his eye. How many people could give of themselves as generously as Hailey did? It made him want to pull her close and hold her tight. He resisted the urge.

"It's getting late," he said, glancing up at the darkening sky. "We should get back."

"Are you okay?" Hailey asked.

"Yeah, I'm fine," Kid lied. "Just fine."

The gray day turned into a rainstorm on the way home. The slap of the windshield wipers kept a steady cadence in time with the drumming of the raindrops on the roof. The cozy atmosphere enveloped the van. Cars whooshed through the rain all around them, but Kid felt as if he and Hailey were apart from the world somehow, separated in their own little cocoon.

He stopped at a red light and glanced at her out of the corner of his eye. She was tracing patterns on the foggy window with the tip of her finger. It looked as if she was drawing a chopper. Not a very good one.

"What are you thinking about?" he asked.

She startled as if he'd awoken her from a dream.

She gave him a small smile. "You were good with the kids today."

"I didn't do anything," he said.

"You got down on their level. You talked to them and joked with them. That means a lot to them."

"You mean a lot to them," he said.

"I guess that's only fair," she said. "They mean a lot to me, too."

"I owe you an apology," he said. "I never appreciated your commitment to those kids or the auction. I misjudged you. I'm sorry."

"Nah," Hailey said and waved a hand at him. "Not necessary."

"Yes, it is," he said.

A car behind them honked. Kid glanced up to find the light was green. If he believed in signs, this would be a hell of a good one.

"Are you hungry?" he asked as he wound his way through the dark, rain-slicked streets toward the garage.

"Actually, yes," she said.

"Want to order a pizza?" he asked.

"Decusatti's?" she asked.

"Is there any other?"

"No anchovies," she said.

"Done," he said as he turned into The Chop Shop's drive and hit the automatic door opener. The door at the far end of the garage swung open and Kid drove in. "Let's unload tomorrow. I want to look at the children's artwork and see what our options are."

HAILEY GRABBED THE ARTWORK out of the back of the van and followed Kid into the break room. He ordered a pizza while Hailey spread the drawings on the table.

She overheard him ask for extra cheese, sausage and half green olive. Not bad.

He joined her by the table and they laid out the sheets of poster board. Kid studied the handprints and turned the sheets around and frowned.

"Is something wrong?" she asked. She really loved the

idea of the bike being covered in the kids' handprints. She'd be crushed if they couldn't use them.

"I'm thinking we can use this one for the tank," he said. "And these other two can make up the fenders."

"So, they're usable?"

"Sure," he said. "I'll bring them to my paint guy tomorrow. This is going to be new for him. It's not flames or a busty babe, but I know he can do it."

Hailey sighed with relief and Kid smiled at her. For the first time, she felt as if he understood why this was so important to her. She wondered if she should have taken him to the hospital sooner, but he may not have been so receptive. Maybe he had just needed to get to know her a little bit.

Yeah, right. If anything, she needed to get to know him a little bit. They'd spent almost every day for the past two weeks together and she felt as if she'd had to pry every nugget of personal information out of him. It was as though shucking an oyster in search of an elusive pearl. She was beginning to get calluses.

Kid switched on the television and reclined on the sofa. He flicked through the channels and then sat up with a jolt. "Hey, I love this movie."

Hailey glanced at the television to see Olivia Newton-John flit across the screen. *"Grease?"* she asked in disbelief. "You like *Grease?"*

"A guilty pleasure," he confirmed and winked at her. The movie cut to a commercial and Kid stood up. "How could I not love a movie that includes songs about fast cars?"

He broke into the character Kenickie's trademark song about his car called "Greased Lightning."

Hailey felt her mouth slide open in disbelief. Kid was singing. Kid had a great voice. Kid was dancing. Man, he could move his hips. Kid was approaching her with a predatory gleam in his eye. She gulped.

"Admit it," he teased her. "You think Travolta was hot."

"I was always a Kenickie sort of a girl," she demurred.

"It was his hot rod, wasn't it?" he asked.

Hailey laughed. Could this be Kid Cassidy, the aloof? Was he perhaps letting her get to know him a little bit?

Kid pulled her close in a waltzy dance move and then spun her out. He was humming, "You're the one that I want," and Hailey felt as if her heart might burst through her chest. He was something else.

7

A FIST POUNDED ON THE DOOR. Kid swirled Hailey into a seat and said, "Don't move. I'll be right back."

She couldn't move even if she wanted to. What was wrong with Kid? Or maybe she should be asking what was *right* with Kid? Since the day they'd met, she'd felt as if he'd been keeping her at arm's length, and that was quite literally true during their brief yet hot kiss. And now here he was with open arms. So much for shucking; her oyster had just popped open on his own.

"You're staring," he said as he brought the pizza over to the coffee table.

"I just can't believe that you know the words to a musical." She rose from her seat and went to the kitchenette to grab some paper plates and napkins. In the little refrigerator, she found two cold beers and brought them over, as well.

"What is so shocking?" he asked. "It's not like you found out I wear women's underwear."

Hailey dropped one of the beer cans and he laughed. "That one is yours. And that was a joke. I don't wear women's underwear unless I lose a bet to Uncle Pete."

"You didn't," she said, sitting on the floor beside him.

"For twenty-four hours," he confirmed.

"Was it…?"

"A thong," he confirmed.

Hailey laughed. She didn't want Kid to think she was

laughing at him, but the thought of Kid wearing butt floss was too much. She tried to contain her laughter, but it just got worse.

"You okay over there?" he asked with a grin.

"Fine," she said, coughing.

"All I can say is after that I no longer find them even remotely sexy. I figure if a woman is willing to wear one of those, she's got issues."

"It's much better to just go free," Hailey agreed.

Kid swiveled his head from the TV to her. He swallowed his bite of pizza with an audible gulp and said, "Are you saying what I think you're saying?"

"It's better to go commando, naked, in the skinny," Hailey said.

"So, you don't wear…?" he said, trailing off.

"Can't stand panty lines." It wasn't a total lie. She'd run out of clean laundry and wasn't wearing any underwear today, but if it made Kid suffer as much as she was then she could live with it.

It was Kid's turn to choke on his beer. Hailey took a self-satisfied bite of pizza. She could feel Kid staring at the back of her jeans.

"Damn," he said.

"What's wrong?" she asked.

"I wish Jamie had been right about me."

"What do you mean?" she asked.

"I wish I could melt things with my eyes," he said, giving her posterior a dark look.

Hailey dropped her pizza back onto her plate. Very quietly, she said, "You can."

Kid stared at her for a long moment. Hailey wondered if maybe she'd gone too far. Maybe Kid wasn't as hot for her as she was for him. Maybe he'd just been letting his guard down and teasing her because now that he had met

the kids, he believed in the charity auction. Maybe it had
nothing to do with her. Maybe he didn't find her even remotely attractive. Oh, hell.

Kid leaned close and kissed her. His mouth was warm
and firm. It was as if this time he was sure of what was
happening. She didn't feel his shoulders stiffen and he
didn't pull back. Instead, he leaned forward until Hailey
was bent back against the couch while Kid kissed her with
a single-mindedness that left her breathless.

She twined her arms about his neck and pulled him
closer. With one hand, Kid reached around her back and
switched off the television with the remote. Now the only
sounds in the room were the rain beating on the windows
and their own labored breathing.

"I don't want any distractions," he whispered in her ear
as his lips trailed along her jaw and back to her mouth.
Hailey shivered, but she wasn't cold.

His tongue ran along the seam of her mouth and she
parted her lips under the pressure of his. He deepened the
kiss until she felt it all the way down to her toes. She had
never been kissed like this. But then, she'd never been
with a bad boy like Kid Cassidy, either.

His fingers grasped the zipper at the front of her coveralls and he tugged it open to her waist. She was wearing
a white tank top beneath her coveralls. Kid ran the tip of
a finger over one of her already tight nipples and he grit-
ted his teeth.

"No bra, either?" he asked with a groan. "You're trying
to kill me."

Hailey hissed as his mouth moved over her skin, pushing her shirt aside to get to her breast. He worked his way
around the fleshy part of her anatomy until he finally
grasped her nipple with his teeth. He was gentle, but the
rasping sensation made Hailey dizzy with desire.

She shifted until she was lying flat on the floor. She wanted to be naked and to feel Kid's weight on top of her, but she wasn't sure how to get there. She reached for him, but he evaded her grasp.

"Oh, no," he said with a shuddering sigh. "If this is going to last, I can't be that close to you yet."

"Why not?" she asked.

"Because I am too excited right now," he said and glanced down.

Hailey looked at the front of his coveralls and said, "Oh. Mr. Happy does appear pretty jolly."

"He's delirious," Kid confirmed.

It was more than a little flattering to get such a physical reaction from Kid Cassidy. He was earthy and wild and, frankly, made her damp in places no other man had been able to stir with just a smile before. It was intoxicating.

She leaned close and whispered in his ear, "So, is that a socket ratchet in your pocket or are you just happy to see me?"

"Keep talking tools, woman, and I might not be able to contain myself," he said teasingly. He yanked some pillows off the couch, placed one beneath her head and lay on the floor beside her.

"Hot wrench," she whispered in the sexiest voice she could muster while she ran a hand up and down his chest. "Air compressor. Ball-peen hammer."

"That does it," Kid said with a grin. He rolled over on top of her and grabbed her hands, holding them up over her head. Then he kissed her. It was slow and wet and incredibly thorough. Hailey found herself arching against him. She couldn't get enough.

With one hand he kept her hands up over her head while his other hand worked its way under her tank top, teasing her with featherlight caresses. Just when Hailey didn't think she could stand anymore, he moved his hand lower into the waistband of her jeans. She gasped and he kissed her. The sensation of his fingers moving against her most sensitive parts was too much. An explosion of delight coursed through her and she cried out his name as her pleasure diminished into soft shudders.

She opened her eyes to find Kid watching her. There was a softness to his features that she had never seen before. His gaze was full of tenderness and warmth. It stole her breath. She wanted him to always look at her just like that.

She kicked off her butt-stomping boots and wriggled out of her coveralls. Then she tugged off her jeans and pulled her tank top over her head. Kid watched silently. The hitch in his breathing and the darkening of his blue eyes were the only signs that she had his full attention. Well, not the only signs.

"Your turn," she said.

"I…ugh…I can't believe I'm going to say this," he said. "But I'm not prepared to do this right now."

Now Hailey did look down at the front of his coveralls. With a concerned frown she said, "That's not prepared?"

Kid shifted under her gaze with a chuckle. "I guess I need to clarify. I have no protection with me."

"That's why your clothes are still on?" she asked.

"Uh…yeah," he said.

"That's so sweet," she said and kissed him on the mouth. "And so unnecessary. Madeline, my overly optimistic friend, has always insisted that I carry protection in my purse just in case I get lucky. I'm feeling very lucky tonight."

Hailey rose and strode over to her locker. She couldn't believe that she felt no shyness with Kid. Normally, she would have wrapped herself up in half of the couch cushions and scuttled away like a crab. Instead, with Kid's hot gaze scorching her every step, she practically skipped to her locker.

She tossed her hair over her shoulder to peek at him. A hair toss. Hailey never did the hair toss. She'd tried it before and it always made her feel like a horse, but with Kid it felt as if it was supposed to. It felt flirtatious.

She grabbed a condom out of her purse and strode back to where Kid was waiting. She tossed it at him.

"Just one?" he asked as he wrapped his fingers around her ankle and then slowly slid his hand up her calf to trace small circles behind her knee.

"I…uh…" Hailey stammered. It was so hard to think when he touched her. "I never thought I'd use the one, never mind carry more."

Kid rose to his knees and pressed his lips against her belly. "Then we'd better make this last."

Hailey shivered. Kid pulled her down to sit across his lap. To be completely naked and sitting on the lap of a man still clothed was the most erotic moment of her life.

His lips parted in a smile, and when he lowered his mouth to her collarbone, Hailey could feel the rough rub of his goatee against her skin. She arched her back, bringing him into full contact with her. This time it was Kid who shuddered.

He moved his lips up her neck and back to her mouth. He pulled her close and kissed her long and deep. Hailey wrapped her legs around his waist and pulled him closer.

Kid circled her back with one arm and with his other hand let his fingers slide into her hair, cradling her head as his mouth moved lower across her exposed skin. Hailey could feel her heart beating hard in her chest. White-hot desire was making her feel fuzzy and disoriented. She wanted him. She wanted all of him.

She reached between them and unzipped the lower part of his coveralls. Kid hissed in surprise. She pushed aside his striped boxer shorts until Kid's penis was free. Then she sat back down and pressed herself against him. Kid groaned.

"Hailey," he said, his voice gritty. "You feel so good."

"So do you," she whispered. "So get naked already."

She slid off his lap and Kid complied with an efficiency that left Hailey in no doubt as to his expertise. She'd seen Kid in nothing but his boxers and a helmet. That had been pretty hot, but Kid naked was spectacular. He was long and lean and muscle-hardened. His fingers were callused from hard work and a small heart was tattooed on his chest. She hadn't been able to see it clearly before and now she wasn't sure she wanted to know. Had Kid been so in love at one time that he had tattooed a woman's name on his chest?

She had to know. She looked closely. Inside the heart was the word *Mom*. Hailey couldn't help it. She laughed.

"This isn't the time a man wants to hear a woman laugh," he said as he rolled on the condom and lay down beside her. "What's so funny?"

She pointed to the tattoo. "That's so sweet."

"Yeah, I'm still paying for that one," he said. "My mother forbade me to get a tattoo when I was seventeen, so I figured she wouldn't be so mad if I got a heart with Mom in it. Wrong."

"Is she still mad?" Hailey asked.

"Oh, yeah," he said. "Sixteen years later and still mad."

"It didn't stop you from getting another," she said as she traced the Celtic band around his arm.

"Nope," he said.

"So you're the wild Cassidy," she said. She envied his ability to defy parental disapproval.

"We're all pretty wild," he said. "Right now, however, I am the incredibly turned-on Cassidy."

Hailey shifted into his arms. Lying length to length completely naked was not only very exciting, it was also incredibly intimate. Hailey didn't feel as if she and Kid were just physically making love. There was an intimacy happening that connected them on an emotional level, as well.

Then Kid slid on top of her and Hailey forgot all about emotions. She wanted to be connected with Kid on the most primal level possible. She wanted to be a part of him. Kid slid into her and she gasped. It was perfect.

Hailey wrapped her legs about his waist, but it didn't stop him from moving. The momentum made her body hum and she tightened her legs about him as her body succumbed to pleasure. She tried to slow it down but she couldn't. The force of it took her breath away and she arched and cried out his name. Kid kissed her hard and held her still while his release followed hers.

They were sticky and sweaty, wedged between the leather couch and the coffee table, and Hailey would gladly have stayed that way all night. Kid was not of the same mind, however.

He reared up onto his heels and pulled her up with him. A tumble of brown hair fell over her eyes and he gently pushed it away.

"Come on," he said and took her hand. He led her into the washroom, which she had forgotten housed a shower. It was handy for the days when he had to leave the garage and go to his accountant's, or so he had told her. She wondered if it was really because he did a lot of this sort of entertaining in the break room.

Uh-oh. She shook her head. That sounded like an insecure thought. And there was nothing to be insecure about.

She and Kid were working on a project together. They weren't dating. There was no reason to feel anything other than lust, and that was all she felt. Or so she kept telling herself.

They climbed into the shower and soaped up together. It was slippery and fun and more than a little wicked. Hailey tried not to dwell on any matters of the heart. She was a woman. She had just made love to a man. That meant her logic factor was seriously skewed. No, it was best just to get soapy with the man, share the only clean towel in the place and then snuggle up on the sofa eating cold pizza and drinking warm beer.

Hailey felt her head wobble just as the midnight movie began. She was so relaxed, but it was time to call it a night and go home to bed.

She uncurled herself from Kid and instantly missed his warmth. They were both wearing their coveralls. He had fallen asleep an hour ago and was snoring softly. She tugged on her boots and crept over to her locker, pulled on her sweatshirt and her helmet and grabbed her purse. She debated leaving a note for Kid, but what would she say? Thanks? It was accurate but seemed insufficient.

Better to say nothing. She didn't want to freak him out. They still had to put the chopper together, and if he thought she was hung up on him, it might make things awkward. No, it was better to play it cool. If the man had any idea how hard her heart hammered when he was near, he'd hop on his Harley and ride for the next time zone.

She let herself out the back door and crossed the dark alley to where she'd parked Madeline's Vespa. Wouldn't Madeline be shocked if she knew what Hailey had spent the evening doing? The thought made her smile. She switched on the engine and picked up her feet and zipped around the end of the building.

A pissed-off man was caught in the glare of her headlight and Hailey slammed on her brakes with a screech. The scooter wobbled on the wet pavement and she almost lost her balance but planted her foot just in time.

"Where do you think you're going?" Kid asked, hands on hips.

"Home," Hailey said as she lifted off her helmet. "Do you have a death wish or something? I almost ran over you."

"So you just leave?" he said. "You don't even say goodbye?"

"You were asleep. I didn't want to wake you."

Kid frowned at her, and in the light of the street lamp, Hailey thought she saw hurt and uncertainty flit through his eyes. It was gone in a flash, but Hailey was sure she'd seen it. It had never occurred to her that Kid would actually care. The thought made her feel warm and regretful. She should have woken him up at least to say goodbye.

"I'm sorry," she said. Then she teased, "You're just so pretty when you're snoring. I couldn't bear to wake you up."

"Snoring?" he scoffed. He looked a teeny bit mollified and turned away from her with a sniff. "I just feel so cheap and used."

Hailey felt a grin part her lips. "Oh, baby," she said. "Don't be like that."

Kid turned back around to face her. His gaze met hers and he said, "What are you going to do to make it up to me?"

The look scorched, and Hailey said the first thing that came to mind. "Anything you want."

Kid grinned. With his thumb, he motioned for her to hop off the scooter. Hailey watched him as he wheeled it into the side door of the garage. She waited and Kid came back out wearing his jacket and helmet and pushing his chopper.

"I'll take you home," he said. "You're not driving that toy on dark roads in the middle of the night."

His voice brooked no argument, but Hailey wasn't intimidated.

"I appreciate the offer," she said. "But how will I get back in the morning if you drop me off tonight?"

"Good point," Kid said. "I guess I'll just have to spend the night at your place and bring you back with me tomorrow."

Hailey's eyes widened and then narrowed with suspicion. Judging by the smile on Kid's face, that had been his plan all along.

"Address?" he asked.

"Fourteen-twelve Elm Street. Just off of First Street in Westport," she said.

"Got it."

Hailey climbed onto the back of his chopper and wrapped her arms about his waist. Kid revved up the motorcycle and they zipped out of the parking lot and onto the road. The rain had stopped but the roads were still slick and shiny. The damp air was cold, and she burrowed into Kid's back for warmth.

Kid was going to spend the night at her place. She tried not to think about the dust bunnies that were large enough to have names and be considered pets. Had she cleaned her bathroom lately? Then again, if she kept Kid distracted, he might not notice. She shivered in anticipation.

Kid was spending the night. She wondered what this meant, if anything. Did it mean they were in a relationship? She suspected he operated a revolving-door policy when it came to women. And apparently Hailey was in the door for the moment. Irene was right. She probably was the flavor of the month. She could see it posted on a white board in a hurried scrawl: Neurotic brunette whose life is a lie. Sprinkles extra.

But the truth was, if she couldn't even tell her parents that she had quit advertising to open a yoga studio, then she could never bring someone like Kid home as her boy-friend. Her mother would have a stroke if she saw his goatee, his earrings and tattoos, never mind the fact that his name didn't start with *Dr.* and that he was essentially a mechanic. The argument that she'd had the best orgasm of her life with him certainly would not be a selling point she could share with her mother.

Kid parked his chopper next to Hailey's Mercedes in the short driveway beside her apartment. Elm was an old street lined with turn-of-the-century brownstones that had long since been converted into two- and three-family houses. Hailey's apartment was the entire second floor, sandwiched between an elderly woman on the first floor and a newly married couple on the third floor. Other than the squeaky bedspring noises heard frequently from above, Hailey had no complaints with her neighbors.

KID FOLLOWED HAILEY UP THE old wooden staircase to the French doors that opened to her apartment. The soft blue glow of a large fish tank lit the sparsely decorated room. An area rug, a futon and a tiny television were the only other pieces of furniture in the room.

"Hi, guys." Hailey made her way to the fish tank. She sprinkled food along the top and the fish scurried up to eat.

Kid knelt beside her to admire the fish. "What are they?"

"Mollies," she said. "I came home with five and within a week someone had babies, and now I have over thirty."

"They look like black velvet," he said.

She beamed at him. "Exactly."

Her hair was a jumble from wearing the helmet, and

traces of whisker burn pinkened her cheeks. She looked so adorably rumpled that Kid couldn't resist. He kissed her. She reacted by wrapping her arms about his neck and pulling him close. It was all the invitation Kid needed.

He deepened the kiss, savoring the taste and smell of her. There was something bewitching about Hailey. She was so earnest and so determined. He admired that. He'd never met a woman who followed through on what she said she was going to do as Hailey did. She said she'd get a chopper for the auction and here she was saving his business so he'd build it for her.

Kid felt more for her than he wanted to acknowledge right now. They were from different worlds and when this project was over, they'd probably find their connection was over, too. But he could no more stop making love to her tonight than he could stop breathing. So he concentrated on the here and now, the feel of Hailey in his arms, the sweet smell of her hair and the hardwood floor beneath his knees.

"You know," he said, pulling back to kiss the line of her neck, "this might be more comfortable in a bed."

"You think?" she asked with a wicked glint in her eye. "I was beginning to think you had a floor fetish."

"Kinky," he said, letting her roll to her feet and pull him up behind her. "But my knees would never last."

"Good thing it's not your knees that I'm interested in," Hailey said. She blushed and Kid grinned. Obviously she wasn't used to being so bold. He liked the combination of sweet and brazen. And he really liked that she felt safe enough to be both with him.

She led him through an empty dining room and into a small hallway that had three doors. All three were open. When Hailey switched on the hall light, Kid saw one room that had mats on the floor and bamboo plants in each corner. Another was a large bathroom with an old claw-footed iron tub. And finally he saw the bedroom. Ah.

He propelled Hailey into that room. It looked like a harem. The walls were gold and the bed was red velvet surrounded by sheer gold curtain. Pillows, also in rich golds and reds, covered the bed.

"Nice," he said.

"I've been watching entirely too many home-improvement shows," she said with a self-conscious laugh. "I wanted a real boudoir and, boy, did I create one."

"I like it," he said. "How do you get in there?"

Hailey opened the netting and climbed onto the bed. Kid followed, and the netting fell back behind them, reminding him of that moment in the van when it had felt like just the two of them in a cocoon. It was exactly how Kid felt when he was with her. Safe.

When she twined her arms about him, Kid felt a sense of completeness he'd never felt before. He pushed it aside. Right now the only thing he wanted to think about was making long, slow, sweet love to Hailey.

HAILEY AWOKE TO FIND A six-foot-one, tattooed biker in her bed. She smiled. She spent the rest of the day smiling, as well.

She and Kid worked side by side on the mock-up of the chopper. They attached all of the parts to the frame. As they worked through it, it all began to make sense to her. She didn't quite grasp the different measurements, like the degree of the rake, but she understood more about belts and pulleys and axle spacers than she'd ever imagined knowing.

It was fun to watch Kid in his element. He hefted their twin-cam engine as if it were nothing. He showed her what a transmission looked like and how the belts all went together. He had Hailey clean up the frame and hammer the parts together. It was grueling, exhausting work, and she loved it. When it was all done, their green-primer-colored chopper with the chrome-colored engine sat expectantly.

Hailey couldn't believe it. They had done it and it was gorgeous. She wanted to jump up and down, but she was too tired.

"Not bad," Chooch said as he ambled over to look at their work. "This is going to be a fine machine."

"You think so?" Hailey asked, feeling ready to bust with pride.

"I know it," Chooch said.

"Tomorrow we send it out for paint," Kid said.

"Hey, are you planning on paying us overtime?" Uncle Pete called across the garage with a teasing grin. "It's past four. I have to go. I have a date."

"Then go," Kid answered. "You're going to need the time to make yourself pretty."

Uncle Pete gave him a sour look.

"Uncle Pete has a girlfriend?" Hailey asked.

"Several," Chooch said.

"Yeah, he's working his way through the senior center. Last year, two of the blue hairs had a catfight over him. They attacked each other with bingo daubers," Kid said. "There were pink and green fluorescent dots everywhere. It was ugly."

Hailey laughed and Kid smiled at her. Their eye contact made her sizzle. She wondered if anyone knew. They'd been very professional at the garage. She had tried to keep the longing looks to a minimum and not blurt out, "Hey, I've seen this man naked" to anyone. But it hadn't been easy.

She glanced at her watch. Uncle Pete was right. It was

getting late. She had two classes to teach tonight, and if she was going to get there on time she had to hurry.

"I have to go," she said. "My other job…"

Her voice trailed off weakly and Hailey could have kicked herself. She sounded weird. All day she had been fine, but now that she was leaving him she sounded weird. Great, just great. So much for her coolness factor.

"I'll walk you out," Kid said. "We need to talk about that…uh…paint thing."

He sounded odd, too. Chooch looked between them and his lips twitched. Jeez, had he figured out that they…? Nah. He couldn't have. Could he?

Kid waited for Hailey to grab her stuff and then walked her over to where they'd left her Vespa the night before.

"I still don't like you driving this thing," he said. "It's too small."

"I'll be fine," Hailey said and slid on her helmet. "At least it's still light out."

An awkward silence settled between them. Hailey wasn't sure what to say and Kid seemed stumped, as well. It was as if they'd been dancing in perfect rhythm and then someone had stomped on someone's foot and they had stumbled to a halt. Hailey wasn't sure if she was the stomper or the stompee.

"I had fun last night," he said.

"Me, too," she said. "We should do it again sometime."

The words were out before she could catch them. Did she sound too desperate? What if it had just been a one-nighter for Kid and now she was turning it into a thing?

"I'd like that," he said and smiled. Then he kissed her. It was short and sweet, but it warmed Hailey all the way down to her toes. Maybe it hadn't been just a one-nighter.

She fired up the Vespa and tried to give a carefree wave,

but she was too self-conscious and it came out awkward. Kid grinned at her and suddenly it didn't matter.

"I BROUGHT YOUR SCOOTER BACK," Hailey said as she rushed into the office.

Madeline was sacked out on the hammock they had strung from wall to wall behind their desks. She looked tired and Hailey felt major guilt. Here she was having fun boinking Kid, and Madeline was working double time to cover for her.

"I'm sorry I've been away so much," Hailey said. "But we're in the home stretch. I swear. We put the mock-up of the chopper together today, and tomorrow it goes out for paint."

"Don't worry. Gladys has picked up most of your classes. She's doing great," Madeline said as she rolled her head toward Hailey and narrowed her eyes. "You look different."

"I've started wearing my hair down," Hailey said quickly.

"That's not it," she said. "Spill."

"There's nothing to spill," Hailey protested, but she couldn't keep the grin off of her face.

"Oh, my God. Did you have another wangdoodle sighting?" Madeline asked as she rolled out of the hammock and leaned forward. She was in optimum gossip stance, like a runner at the gate.

"Uh-huh." Hailey nodded and felt her face grow hot. "And then some."

"You slept with him?" Madeline's mouth formed a perfect O and her eyes widened.

"Uh-huh." Hailey nodded again.

"Right on!" Madeline shouted and pumped a fist. "So much for your hot-manaphobia. So...how was it?"

Hailey opened her mouth but nothing came out. How could she describe what she had shared with Kid?

"That good?" Madeline asked with a note of awe in her voice.

"Yeah," Hailey said. "I have no idea what's going to happen, but I wouldn't trade last night for anything."

"Wow," Madeline breathed.

"Yeah," Hailey agreed.

The Flintstones's "Yabba Dabba Do" theme chimed, jarring the women out of their mutual daydreams.

"Oh, you left your cell phone here and your mother has been calling every half hour since noon."

"Hmm." Hailey felt her stomach tighten. "This can't be good news. Did she say why she was calling?"

"What am I, crazy? I didn't talk to her," Madeline said. "I just looked at the readout to see if it was you."

Hailey opened her desk drawer and reached for her liter bottle of antacid. She wondered what her mother was worried about. Oh, man, what if someone had spotted her at the rally or on the back of Kid's chopper last night? How could she explain?

It was best to get it over with. She picked up the phone and said, "Hello."

"Hailey, is that you?" her mother gasped.

"Yes, Mother, it's me," Hailey said. "Sorry I missed your call. What can I do for you?"

"That's *calls*, dear," Selma said. "I must have called you seven times. Where were you?"

"Working on…the…uh…auction," Hailey said. Not a total lie. "I had some details to work out with Mr. Cassidy."

Madeline snorted and made an obscene gesture with her hands. Hailey turned her back on her before she laughed. Why couldn't Madeline have been Selma's daughter? She could have steamed the starch out of Selma's panties. Unlike Hailey, who chafed as if she were wearing them herself.

"That's nice, dear," Selma said. "But I have interesting news. Dr. Burke is in town, and he called here looking for you—"

"Burke called for me?" Hailey interrupted. She turned back around and made bug eyes at Madeline, who returned the look. "But why?"

"Well, he didn't tell me," Selma said with a sniff that let Hailey know how she felt about that. "But he seemed very eager, and if my intuition is correct—and it usually is—I suspect there's a proposal in the offing. Isn't that exciting?"

"You have no idea, Mother," Hailey said. "Truly, no idea."

8

HAILEY FELT AS IF SHE WERE in a covert operation. She had no idea why Burke was looking for her, but she had no intention of running into him. She stealthily crept from her apartment to her car, as if Burke might be in the bushes waiting to pounce. Probably he was just being polite to make up for having his housekeeper dump her like yesterday's trash while he pulled up stakes and moved to Boston without so much as a "See you around." Probably he felt guilty about it and wanted to apologize. Probably.

But then there was this one nagging voice in Hailey's head that said maybe he was here to get her back. She tried not to listen to it. She tried to tell it to go away. But there it was, the first level of paranoia in her newfound happiness. She'd finally found someone that she adored and that made her feel wonderful, but who happened to be totally unacceptable to her parents, especially her mother. And then—bang—the man her mother salivates over is back in town looking for her. It had to be the cosmic ass-kicking of the year.

Hailey drove straight to the garage. She parked on a side street and walked over. She saw Uncle Pete in the break room. He was reading the paper and sipping coffee from a cardboard cup from Hank's Diner.

Hailey wondered if he knew about her and Kid. She wondered if he approved. He was a real live wire, and his devotion to Kid was obvious. She liked him and wanted him to approve.

"'Morning," she said as she entered the room. Uncle Pete looked up from his paper and gave her a warm smile.

"Well, it sure is nice to see a pretty girl in the morning instead of the usual suspects," he said and went back to his paper. Hailey noticed it was the editorial section. Somehow she'd expected it to be the funnies.

"Thanks, Pete," she said. She strode over to her locker, dumped her bag and pulled on her coveralls. There was the distinct smell of feet in the air and she wondered which one of the guys hadn't cleaned his locker lately.

She reached back into her bag and pulled out a sachet of potpourri. It was a lovely vanilla-lavender scent, just the thing to dispel the pungent odor of men. There were no bowls in the kitchenette cupboards, just paper plates and cups. Hailey looked over at the trophy case. One of those would do nicely. She found the trophy with the biggest bowl and dumped the potpourri into it. The air was fresher in minutes. Pleased with herself, she went to admire the mock up of the chopper.

She knew that they had to break it down today to get the frame, tank and fenders in for paint. She decided to start the dismantling herself, working in the opposite order of the way they'd put it together yesterday. She could do this. Absolutely.

KID WALKED INTO THE SHOP A half hour earlier than usual. It had nothing to do with wanting to see Hailey, or so he kept telling himself. He refused to acknowledge the fact that he had missed her last night.

"Is Hailey here yet?" he asked Uncle Pete, who was engrossed in the paper.

"She's in the garage," Uncle Pete said. "And hello to you, too."

"Uh, sorry. It's just that I want to make sure we get the mock-up taken down and ready for paint." It sounded lame even to him, but Kid hoped Uncle Pete wouldn't call him on it. He wasn't ready to discuss what was happening with Hailey yet.

"So, have you signed on with that new team yet, or are you waiting for a better contract?" Uncle Pete asked.

Ah, the old sports analogy for love-life gossip that he and Pete always used to discuss their dealings with women. This he could handle.

"I'm waiting for the new team to make an offer," he said. "I'm still not sure I'm in their league, although I've spent some quality time in the batting cage."

"Good way to play it," Pete said, finally lowering the paper and looking him in the eye. "A smart team would snap you up, and I think you've got a smart team on your hands."

"Hmm." Kid hummed. He didn't want to think about the alternative—that the team might pass on him. "Do you smell something?"

Pete sniffed the air. "Just my coffee. Why?"

"Something smells funny," Kid said and shrugged and then he made his way out to the garage.

"Argh!" Hailey growled and then stomped the cement floor with her foot. Her face was red and she was straining with exertion. Dismantling the mock-up was not going well for her.

Kid had a nice view of her profile. She had a stubborn chin, and a strand of hair was stuck to her cheek by a smear of grease. Her coveralls aptly covered all of her curves, but that was all right because he had them memorized. The desire to see those curves again hit him hot and hard. He sucked in a breath. Peaches had really done a number on him.

As if she sensed his presence, she turned to face him. Her lips curved in a beaming smile that toasted him more warmly than a cup of hot cocoa on a winter's day. He would have happily gone bobbing for marshmallows right then and there if her smile hadn't suddenly collapsed into a frown.

"You know, when I was in advertising, I could sell anything to anyone," she said. "I was good, really good."

"So that's where the Mercedes came from?" he asked.

"Uh-huh," she said. "I thought it would make me happy."

"It didn't?" he asked.

"It's a Mercedes," she said. "Of course it did."

She grinned and Kid laughed.

"So why did you quit?" he asked.

"I was too successful," she said, waving a wrench at him. "It started to mess up my life."

"And you're telling me this because…" Kid wondered if this was her lead-in to dumping him. Great, a woman who charms while she dumps—just what he needed.

"Why is it I could be responsible for millions of dollars but I can't get this miserable bolt to budge?" she asked.

Kid squinted at the bolt. "Did you try going in the other direction?"

"No, I…" Hailey's voice trailed off and she turned away from him.

He watched her fiddle with the tank, and sure enough, she turned back around triumphantly with the bolt in hand. You'd think she'd just taken the gold for the Olympic decathlon. It gave Kid an even warmer feeling than before, and he absolutely refused to think about it.

"Let's get to work," he said and joined her at the mock-up.

Two hours later, it was disassembled. Chooch loaded it into the van and Kid and Hailey drove it to Kid's paint guy in Milford.

Justin, the paint guy, sported two sleeves of tattoos on his arms, several earrings and a square patch of hair on his chin, but he still looked twelve instead of twenty-four.

Hailey tried not to stare.

"Don't worry," Kid said. "He's the best."

Kid and Justin discussed the artwork while Hailey examined the work space. It was an old warehouse that reeked of paint. She wondered how Justin could work here and not have a perpetual headache.

Motorcycle frames and tanks and fenders hung from the ceiling in every hue imaginable. Some had fancy scrollwork and some had shooting flames. One even had a portrait of Betty Page, the famous fifties pinup girl. Hailey felt herself relax. If Justin could do that then he could handle hers.

"This is going to be sweet," Justin was saying as Hailey joined them. "And for a cause, too. Right on."

"I need it by Tuesday morning," Kid said. "Can you do that?"

"Sure. Wednesday at the latest," Justin said.

Kid smiled. "So, I'll pick it up Tuesday morning."

Justin returned the smile. "Tuesday morning."

The ride back to the garage was quiet. Hailey wasn't sure what to say. Kid had kissed her when she'd left the garage yesterday but now she didn't know if that had been an I-like-you-let's-keep-seeing-each-other kiss or a last-night-was-fun, kiss-off kiss. She'd gotten no signals whatsoever from him today.

"Are you teaching again tonight?" Kid asked, breaking the silence.

"Two classes," Hailey said. "One at six and one at seven-thirty."

Kid turned into The Chop Shop's lot. "That's a long day for you, isn't it?"

"It's not too bad, really," she said, wondering where this was going.

"I was thinking…" Kid parked the van next to a BMW and turned to face her.

Hailey felt her breath catch as she recognized the BMW. Burke! How could he have found her?

"I've got to go," she said to Kid and leaped out of the van. She scanned the parking lot but there was no sign of Burke. Oh, man, where was he?

Just then she saw him striding across the lot carrying two cups of coffee. She ducked into one of the open garage doors. Mikey said hello. She ignored him and spied around the wall. Burke was talking to Kid.

Where to hide? She lurched across the garage and into the break room. She yanked open the bathroom door to find Chooch there, obviously finishing up some personal business as he stood by the sink washing his hands.

"Out. Out. Get out. Get out," Hailey said and she ripped off a ream of paper towels from the dispenser, shoved them into Chooch's hand and pushed him out the door.

"Dang," Chooch muttered as she shut the door behind him. "Ever heard of knocking?"

Hailey turned the deadbolt and collapsed against the door. There was no way Burke could find her in here. But what if he waited? What if Kid told him that she'd run to the bathroom and Burke decided to wait? She couldn't hide in here all night. Or could she? Hailey paced around the square little room.

It was almost three o'clock. The shop closed at four. Surely Burke wouldn't wait that long. She should just face him and get it over with. What was the big deal? Even if he was here looking to rekindle their romance, she didn't have to go along with it. She could say, "no, thank you." Yeah, sure. Passing on a pediatrician would kill her mother.

Hailey felt her stomach knot up. She had to face the fact that what she wanted and what her mother wanted were two different things. The nausea hit her hard, and Hailey sat down and put her head between her knees.

This was ridiculous. She was twenty-nine years old. She was a partner in a successful business and she had found a man who she really lo…liked. There was no reason to feel sick to her stomach at the thought of disappointing her mother. Her brother Jack never did. But then, her mother's expectations of Jack were different. While Hailey was to marry a doctor and be a pillar of society, Jack needed merely to stay out of jail and not bring home a hooker.

Hailey rolled to her feet and splashed cold water on a cloth. She slapped it on her forehead and gazed at herself in the mirror. She looked like something the tide had brought in and left on the beach to rot.

A fist banged on the door and Hailey jumped.

"Hailey, are you all right?" Kid asked.

"Fine," she squeaked. "I'm fine."

"Are you planning on coming out?" He didn't sound amused. "It is the only facility, you know."

"Um, did you need me for something?" she asked. If he said yes, then she was definitely not coming out!

"No, but Uncle Pete is out here doing the pee-pee dance," Kid said. "Could you hurry up before he has an accident?"

"Oh!" Hailey unlocked the door and yanked it open. "I'm sorry."

Kid grabbed her hand and pulled her all the way out.

"Hey, where is Uncle Pete?" she asked.

"What are you hiding from?" he asked.

"Nothing," she said. "Did you just lie to get me out of there?"

"Fibbed," he conceded. "So, what's going on?"

"Nothing," she said. "Can't a girl use the rest room for…uh…girl stuff?"

"For thirty minutes?" he asked doubtfully. "Your friend with the Beemer left fifteen minutes ago."

"He's not my friend. What makes you think he's my friend?" Hailey asked, trying to look merely curious instead of paranoid. By the narrowing of Kid's eyes, she suspected she was failing miserably.

"Who said it was a he?" he asked.

"It wasn't?" she asked, blinking.

Kid looked away and sniffed the air as if he smelled something peculiar. Then he turned back to Hailey. "What's going on?"

"Nothing," she insisted. "So there was a woman?"

"Yes, both," Kid answered. He walked away from her and sniffed the air again. He glanced about them as if he were looking for something.

"Both?" Hailey asked. "So there was a man and a woman here?"

"Yup," he answered, still looking about them. He walked toward the kitchenette and started sniffing around.

"What did they want?" Hailey asked, following him.

"You."

"Me? What for?"

"I don't know," he said. "They didn't say."

"Well, what did you tell them?" she asked.

"That you were out." He looked at her and then he leaned close and sniffed her.

"Why did you tell them that?" she asked.

"You saw that car and ran out of the van like you were on fire," he said. "I figured you didn't want to see whoever it was."

He leaned close and sniffed her again.

"What are you doing?" Hailey asked as she pushed him away.

"Something smells funny and it's driving me nuts," he said.

"I don't smell anything," she said.

"It's flowery," he said. "It smells like my grandmother on Sunday, overpowering."

Uh-oh. Hailey glanced at the trophy case. Kid followed her gaze.

"What did you do?" he asked as he stomped toward the case.

"Nothing much," she squeaked.

Kid started sniffing around his trophies until he found the one filled with potpourri. He sniffed it and then wrinkled his nose in distaste.

"What is this stuff?" he asked.

"Potpourri," she said. "Basically, an air freshener."

"More like an air spoiler," he said. He strode over to the kitchenette and dumped the potpourri in the trash. "Bleck."

"Fine. I suppose you prefer the smell of old socks and armpits," she said, feeling snippy.

"It's better than that sissy stink," he said. "This is a garage. It's supposed to smell like a garage. And since we're on the subject of your improvements, what are these?"

Kid stomped over to the coffee table and held up one of the cork coasters Hailey had brought in last week in a futile attempt to stop the water stains the men were making on the table.

"Coasters," she said. "And don't tell me they're for sissies. They're practical."

"They're silly," he said. "Get rid of them."

"But that lovely table is getting ruined," she protested. "It's going to need refinishing if you keep putting drinks directly on it."

"You are only here to work on a chopper for charity," he said. "You are not here to decorate or deodorize."

"Fine," she said. "I suppose a man of your refined taste knows how a garage should look and smell."

"What's the matter?" Kid asked. "Am I not as refined as your friend, Beemer Boy?"

"Just because he asked for me doesn't make him my friend," she said. "What's wrong with you?"

"Nothing much," he said. "It's just that I was about to ask you out for a real date and you bolt from the van as if you're afraid to be seen with me. Then this yup from Beantown is hot to find you, but he won't tell me why. So, I have to ask myself, what is she hiding? So, you tell me, Hailey, what's going on?"

"You were going to ask me out? On a real date?" she asked.

"Yeah," he admitted grudgingly.

Hailey thought he looked cute when he was annoyed. "I accept."

"I haven't asked you yet," he reminded her.

"So what are we going to do?" she continued, ignoring him. "What should I wear?"

"I was thinking dinner and a movie," he said.

"As in, a restaurant and then the Cineplex?" she asked.

"Unless you'd prefer a bucket of chicken and a rented porno at my place?" he asked with a devilish smile.

"That could be fun," she said, feeling breathless.

Kid shook his head at her. "I'll pick you up at your studio at eight-thirty."

"Make it nine. I'll need to change after class."

"I'll make it eight-thirty and I'll help you," he said with a wink.

Hailey felt her body flush with heat. "Then we'll never make it to the movie."

Kid grinned and turned to walk back into the garage. Halfway there he spun back and asked, "So, who was he?"

"An ex-boyfriend," Hailey said. "Sort of."

"Sort of?" he asked.

"It never went very far," she said. "You could say my career success drove him away."

"Poor bastard," he said with a shake of his head and a phony look of sympathy on his face.

The door closed behind him and Hailey sank into a chair with a sigh. There was no question that Kid Cassidy made her feel like a truly desirable woman. And she liked it. She really, really liked it.

HAILEY WATCHED KID THROUGH the office window that looked into the garage. He was working on the electrical system of another chopper with Chooch. He glanced up and their eyes met, and Hailey felt that wonderful spark sizzle between them.

He winked, letting her know he felt it, too, and then he went back to work. Hailey tried not to stare at him. She really did, but she just couldn't seem to get enough of him today.

Last night had been the most romantic date of her life. They'd had dinner at a quiet seafood restaurant on the shore and then went to see a movie, a comedy. The dinner was fine, but she couldn't even remember what she'd ordered. The movie was funny, but she truthfully couldn't remember the plot. But she could remember sharing a bucket of heavily buttered popcorn with Kid. She could remember the feel of his hand enfolding hers and she could remember the steady pressure of his shoulder against hers as they'd sat pressed together in front of the large screen.

After the movie, they had gone back to Kid's place. Hailey had expected the single-guy equivalent of the garage. Wrong. Kid lived on the shore in an old Victorian captain's house.

It was a work in progress. Walls were missing and there was a huge hole in the kitchen floor. But it was going to be beautiful when it was finished. The master bedroom had a balcony with French doors that opened out onto the water. Hailey and Kid had made love watching the moonlight glimmer on the water below them. Hailey had fallen asleep in Kid's arms, lulled by the sound of the waves. It was as perfect an evening as she could ever remember. And she'd never wanted it to end.

"Hey, you're daydreaming," Kid growled into her ear as he sat down on the edge of her desk.

"I was remembering last night," she said, feigning a peeved expression. "You lied to me."

Kid raised his black eyebrows and scratched his goatee with consideration. "Let's see, I told you I wanted to make love to you and I did, so that's not it."

"Nope, that's not it," she confirmed.

"I told you you were beautiful and you are, so that's not it."

Hailey felt herself blush. She could only imagine where this was going next.

"I told you I wanted to…"

Hailey clapped a hand over his mouth. She had a hot feeling coursing through her that told her if he finished his sentence, she'd be relieving him of his coveralls and having her way with him right there in the garage.

"I'm talking about the feline," she said. "You said you had no pets and yet a cute, fuzzy and fat orange tabby tried to oust me out of your bed this morning as if I was in her spot. So, who is she?"

"He," Kid said. "And he's not mine."

"Who does he belong to, then?" she asked.

"I don't know but he's not mine," he said. "I merely let the Chubman crash at my place when he's in the hood."

"And that would be once or twice a week?" she asked.

"Yeah." Kid looked down and mumbled, "Or daily."

"You are such a softy." Hailey tsk-tsked, thoroughly charmed by this gentle side of Kid. "He's got you wrapped around his little orange paw."

Kid shrugged, looking chagrined.

"So, why do you call him Chubman?" she asked.

"He was a skinny little runt when he first showed up. I figured if I called him Chubby, Chubman, Chubster or a variation of those, he'd plump up."

"It seems to have worked," Hailey said with a laugh. "What's he weigh?"

"Fifteen pounds," Kid said as he coughed into his hand. "Hey, you're one to talk. I saw those fish. You could have a fish fry over there and no one would go hungry."

Hailey gasped, "My babies! You just keep the Chubman from fishing in my tank."

Kid wiggled his eyebrows. "How about me? Can I fish in your tank?"

Hailey giggled then looked appalled.

"Oh, man, did I just giggle? Sheesh, I'm embarrassing myself."

"So, I leave for a couple of days and you replace me with some bimbo that you're doing the bang tango with? Great. That's loyalty for you."

Hailey swiveled around to see an irate man standing in the doorway. He was sporting a dark tan, khaki shorts and a loud Hawaiian shirt with flip-flops.

"Stan, we thought you were dead," Kid said. "Let me introduce Hailey, who is volunteering her services here while we build her a chopper for charity."

"Charity?" Stan stepped into the room. "What's going on? I got your message. It said you hired a replacement for me. If it isn't her then who is it?"

"No, on the fiftieth message—and yes, that is an accurate count—I said that we had a woman helping out who had managed to sell over a dozen choppers in the past week and a half and that if you didn't come back, we may just keep her," Kid said. "Does Irene know you're back?"

"No," Stan said. "It's complicated."

"What about our former office girl, Marie?" Kid asked. "Did she come back with you?"

"No." Stan ran a hand over his receding hairline. "She stayed in Belize."

Kid looked at him.

"She dumped me for a bartender, okay?" Stan snapped. Kid nodded.

"I need to talk to you," Stan said to Kid and nodded his head in the direction of Kid's office.

Kid turned away from him and back to Hailey.

"I suppose I have to let you go to that charity lunch meeting that you're supposed to attend?" he asked.

"Yes, at noon," Hailey said. "I'm leaving at eleven-thirty."

"Make that eleven-forty-five," Kid said and pointed to the clock.

"What?" Hailey leaped to her feet. She tore the bandanna from her hair and unzipped her coveralls, shoving them down to her ankles without taking her boots off. Stepping on the pant legs, she tried to hop out of the coveralls without falling. She was going to be late. Her mother was going to be furious. "Oh, no. Oh, crap."

"Peaches." Kid grabbed her upper arms and held her still. Then he carefully untangled her from the coveralls. "It's okay. You're going to be a little late, but I'm sure everyone will understand."

"Everyone but my mother," Hailey said. "Oh, brother, my mother."

She pecked Kid on the cheek and then raced to her car, leaving him shaking his head in her wake.

HAILEY TUGGED OFF HER BOOTS and jeans at the first red light. The second light was green. Naturally it was, because she could have actually used the thirty seconds to pull on her pantyhose. There was never a red light when you needed one.

She stopped at a stop sign and pulled on her hose, trying not to cause a run. The car behind her honked and Hailey jumped, shoving her big toe right through the hose. Damn. She wiggled into the rest of the hose, hoping her shoe would cover the hole. The driver behind her swung around her car, giving her a nasty look as he went.

Hailey pulled on her straight gray skirt and reminded herself to breathe. She was only five minutes late so far. Maybe her mother wouldn't notice.

Just before the turn into her parents' drive, Hailey pulled over and slouching low in her seat, switched her halter top for the conservative white blouse her mother preferred. A car full of teenage boys shouted as they passed, leaving Hailey in no doubt that they had seen her in just her bra. A few weeks ago she would have been mortified, but right now she really didn't care. She tugged on her stiff gray jacket and ran her fingers through her hair before rocketing up her parents' driveway.

"Late again?" Selma asked with her eyebrows raised disapprovingly.

"I'm sorry, Mother," Hailey said as she opened the passenger door. "I was caught late at work."

"I don't know why you insist on working so hard," Selma said, fussing with her chartreuse blouse that sported a purple silk begonia the size of her head on her left shoulder. "With Dr. Burke about to propose, I would think you should quit working to start planning your wedding. It's going to take us at least a year to work out all of the details. And of course you'll move home so we can work on it together."

Hailey had to lock her knees to keep from keeling over. Her stomach gave a lurch and she felt dizzy.

"Mother, Burke hasn't proposed yet," Hailey said. "In fact, I haven't even seen him since he's been back."

"Not to worry," Selma said. "I'm sure he has had some family obligations. After all, he did call looking for you first and foremost, so I'm sure it's just a matter of time. You must make sure you are presentable at all times. Speaking of which, did you know you had a run? How many times have I told you that you really should carry a spare pair of hose for emergencies?"

Selma pointed at her leg and Hailey sighed. Two inches of a tiny run was showing.

Her mother actually believed Burke was going to propose. Just the thought made Hailey queasy. The valet took the keys to her car and Hailey trailed behind her mother as they made their way to the Sunshine Room, where the other ladies were waiting.

"Selma and Hailey," Caroline greeted them at the door with a warm smile. "It's so good to see you. Let's enjoy lunch and then we'll go over the final details. Can you believe the big event is just a week away?"

Hailey followed her mother to the large table, already set for lunch. Most of the seats were taken, and to Hailey's relief, there weren't two seats together. She and her mother would have to sit apart. Selma frowned at her, letting her know that she wasn't pleased and that she held Hailey personally responsible for making them late.

Hailey braced herself for a bout of guilt, but to her surprise, her own relief outweighed any guilt she might have felt. Taking a seat opposite her mother, she eyeballed the food tray before her. She passed over the yucky watercress and grabbed the last cheese croissant. This day was looking up.

"Hailey, I was wondering if I could impose upon you for a favor," Caroline said, resuming her place in the seat beside her.

"Sure," Hailey said. She swallowed her bite of sandwich in an awkward gulp.

"Mr. Cassidy's donation is one of the largest we've ever received," Caroline said. "Since you were the point of contact, I was wondering if you'd bring him to the auction. I'd like to see that he gets the acknowledgment he deserves. Besides, I hear he's really cute."

"He is," Hailey said. "I'd be happy to bring him. Actually, I'd been planning to all along."

"Oh?" Caroline blinked. "Are you two…?"

Hailey glanced at her mother, who was frowning and watching their conversation intently as if trying to read their lips.

"Uh, no," she said. "He's just a very nice man."

"Well, terrific. I look forward to meeting him," Caroline said.

She turned back to the rest of the table with her bubbly warmth, but Hailey felt as if she'd just been locked in a deep freeze. Being dishonest about her feelings for Kid made her feel lower than dirt. Amazingly, it was worse than the usual stomach cramps that pained her when she disappointed her mother. Perhaps, she thought, because it hurt higher up, closer to her heart.

The women took turns reporting on the state of the charity auction. Decorations were in order. Tickets for the event were almost sold out. Big-name entertainment had been lined up. And the auction items had been gathered. With only a few twinges of nerves, Hailey promised that Kid would deliver the chopper just before the auction. Then she said a silent prayer that they got it done on time.

"So now the big question is—" Caroline paused and glanced around the table for dramatic effect "—what is everyone wearing?"

Everyone began to talk at once. Everyone but Hailey. She had no idea what she was going to wear. Honestly, she didn't really care. This wasn't supposed to be about designer gowns and a blurb in the society pages. This was supposed to be about helping the children, like Matty and Jamie. For a second, she pictured attending the ball in her coveralls or, even better, the outfit she'd worn to the biker rally.

"What's so funny, Hailey?" Caroline asked.

Hailey thought about lying but didn't. "I was trying to picture attending the auction dressed as a biker chick."

"A biker chick?" Selma repeated as if Hailey had suggested they go nude.

Caroline burst out laughing. "Oh, wouldn't that be hilarious? We should do it."

Selma looked appalled.

"How exactly does a biker chick look?" asked one of the older ladies.

"Bikini tops and do-rags and very short shorts with boots," Hailey answered. All eyes turned to look at her. "Or so I've heard."

"Charming," Selma said. Her tone made it clear she didn't find it charming in the least.

"Well, I guess that idea is out," Caroline said, correctly interpreting the frowns of the older ladies on the committee. Then she winked at Hailey. "But it would have been funny."

"It is a black-tie event," Selma said. "Full-length gowns are required." She glared at Audry, who'd had the audacity to wear a cocktail dress the year before.

"I don't know, I kind of like the idea of wearing a bikini top," Audry said. "And maybe some black leather chaps."

Two spots of red appeared on Selma's cheeks. Hailey felt her stomach twinge. This wasn't good. It was time to defuse the potentially icky scene that was coming.

"Where were you thinking of going shopping, Mother?" Hailey asked. "Maybe I could go with you and you could advise me."

"You don't have your dress yet?" Selma asked in alarm. "Hailey, what have you been doing with your time? You should have had your dress weeks ago. We'll go straight after lunch."

Hailey glanced over at Audry. The desire to strangle her was almost more than she could stand. To her credit, Audry looked appropriately contrite. Hailey took a bite of her cheese croissant. It was going to be a long day.

"WHAT THE HELL IS THAT?" Madeline screeched and leaped out of her seat and backed away when Hailey pulled her gown out of its bag and hung it on a hook in their office.

"My gown for the charity auction," Hailey sighed

"Oh, you didn't," Madeline said with a shake of her head.

"Didn't what?" Hailey asked.

"Go shopping with your mother," Madeline said. "I thought we made a deal that you were never to shop with her ever again under any circumstance, including losing your entire wardrobe to fire, flood or any other natural disaster."

"I had to go," Hailey said. "There was about to be an incident."

"What color is that exactly?" Madeline asked.

"Pink, sort of," Hailey said.

"And are those…?"

"Feathers? Yes, they are," Hailey said, looking at the dress and feeling ill. "White feathers on a hot-pink bodice and underskirt. If I flap hard enough, I'm pretty sure I can spend the winter in Brazil. Maybe I'd fit in there during the carnival season."

Madeline approached the dress as if she were afraid it would bite or, at the very least, peck her. She whistled.

"And I thought the orange-sherbet suit was bad," she said. "Honey, great hair and makeup can't even get you out of this one."

"It gets worse," Hailey said.

"It comes with matching shoes and a purse?" Madeline asked in horror.

"My mother thinks it is the perfect dress to accept a proposal in," Hailey said. "Apparently Burke is going to be at the auction, and my mother has convinced herself that he is going to propose."

"But aren't you going with Kid?" Madeline asked.

"Yes, I am," Hailey said, although her voice faltered a little bit. "I am. I just have to ask him first."

9

HAILEY FINISHED HER SHIFT AT the Children's Hospital with a rousing session of music with the kids. They pretended to be a rock band, and Hailey got to be the drummer. It was certainly therapeutic to bang out all of her anxiety on a toy drum set.

She wondered how things were going between Kid and Stan, suspecting Kid was going to give Stan another chance. She admired his ability to forgive his partner.

She was smiling as she headed down the hallway when she heard a familiar voice at the nurse's station.

"Hi, Amy. It's nice to see you."

It was Burke. Hailey froze and hugged the wall, trying to look like a brick and blend in.

"Dr. Masterson, it's great to see you again," Amy said. "We heard you were in town."

"Amy, does Hailey Fitzwilly still volunteer here?" he asked.

"Every Friday," Amy said. "Weren't you two…oops, sorry, none of my biz."

"No, that's all right," Burke said. "We were until I goofed it up. I'd really like to see her again. Is she here now?"

"She should be finishing up in the activity room," Amy said.

"Great. I'll go see if I can catch her."

Eek! He was coming this way. Hailey scanned for an escape route—a door, a window, a hole in the ground. He'd said he wanted to see her again. Oh, no, did he mean see her or *see* her?

A lone cart stood at the end of the hall. Hailey ducked behind it, grabbed the sheet that covered the cart and dove beneath it. This was what the kids affectionately called "the poop cart." The smell hit her right between the nostrils. It was full of used bedpans on their way to be sterilized.

Hailey gagged but then she heard footsteps. She breathed through her mouth, hoping she wouldn't heave up her grilled-cheese-sandwich-and-tomato-soup lunch. The sound of the footsteps slowly faded around the corner, and Hailey limply crawled out from under the sheet and scurried down the hall.

Bedpans. Well that was certainly an apt description for her relationship with Burke. Whenever he was around, she ended up in deep sh…

"Hailey," Amy greeted her as she came around the corner. "Dr. Masterson was just looking for you."

"He was?" Hailey asked. "Too bad I missed him. Got to run. The charity auction is next week. So much to do."

"Yeah," Amy said with a snort. "Like curl up in bed for the weekend with your new hottie."

"Kid's not my—" Hailey began, but Amy interrupted. "Oh, please. I've seen you two together. I also saw that billboard of him on I-95." She fanned herself. "He is hot!"

"Yeah," Hailey agreed. Well, she couldn't argue with that.

"My hub saw the billboard and he said it was just the chopper. He said they could put any man, even him, on the chopper and he'd look just as good. I told him they'd only put him on the billboard if he was *under* the chopper." Amy laughed and Hailey joined her. "Go home and enjoy that man."

"You know, that sounds like a plan. See you."

Amy was a genius, Hailey thought as she raced to her car. What better way to avoid Burke than to hide out at Kid's for the weekend. Mrs. Henry from downstairs could feed her fish. Then she'd just have to avoid him a few more days and by the time Burke caught up to her, she'd be on Kid's arm at the auction. And Burke wouldn't dare approach her then. Right? It wasn't much of a plan, but it was all she had. And she was more than willing to sacrifice herself in Kid's bed for the next three days if that's what it took.

"Peaches, wake up," Kid said as he nuzzled the soft spot under her ear.

"Nunh," was her dull response. He trailed his lips down her neck and across her shoulder.

"Hailey, it's Tuesday. We can pick up the tank and fenders today."

Hailey snapped up to a sitting position, dislodging Kid and forcing him to grip the edge of the mattress.

"Why didn't you say so?" she asked. She hopped off of the bed and scurried around the room gathering her clothes.

Kid lay in bed watching her until Hailey was forced to look up and say, "What? Why aren't you moving?"

"I'm enjoying the peep show," he said.

"Really?" she asked. "After this weekend, I'm pretty sure I don't have an inch of skin that you haven't seen."

"It's more than that. You make me happy," he said. He'd said it quietly with his gaze locked on hers. He cared. It made Hailey feel light-headed—in a good way.

"I care about you, too."

They looked at one another for a long moment. For now, it was enough.

"So, why are you standing all the way over there?" he asked and waved her back to the bed with him.

Hailey strolled over, letting the tension build between them. Then she leaned toward him and gave him a big shove. Kid landed on the floor with a thump.

"Get moving," she said and hurried back toward the bathroom.

Kid frowned at her from the other side of the bed. "Very cute. You'd better make some room in that shower, Peaches, because I'm a big believer in water conservation."

HAILEY FELT AS IF EVERYTHING was going her way. The newly painted parts looked terrific in bright yellow with the children's handprints covering the gas tank, fenders and matching yellow frame. There had never been a chopper like this one. She had a great feeling about it. It was going to make a fortune for the hospital and she had done it. As she helped tighten the tranny bolts so that they could install the shocks, she had never felt prouder of anything in her life.

She had walked away from the wreckage of her career in Manhattan and started her own business, and now she was helping to build up a chopper business. Maybe it was her destiny. Maybe she still wanted to be in the advertising game, but marketing the sort of products she wanted to market.

She wondered what her parents would think if they knew of all she had accomplished. Her father would probably be proud, but her mother would be horrified. None of this was a part of Selma's plan for Hailey. Selma wanted for Hailey what she had never had herself—acceptance.

Selma had married up when she'd married Hailey's father, and his family and their cronies had never let her forget it. Despite hobnobbing with the elite for charity events, Selma had never quite been able to break into their inner circle. She wanted Hailey to marry well because she never wanted Hailey to feel the slights she had. Ironically, Hailey didn't care. She chose her friends because of who they were, not what family they were born into. Her mother would never understand this. In her mind, Hailey marrying Burke would finally break down the barriers that had kept her out of the elite's elite world. Too bad it was never going to happen.

A twinge of guilt cramped Hailey's conscience and her stomach burbled. She would like to be honest with her parents and say, "Accept me for who I am," but she was loath to disappoint her mother. She couldn't even imagine what her mother would say at the sight of Kid.

He had facial hair and tattoos and built choppers for a living. Selma would freak.

"Hey, Peaches, why are you frowning?" Kid asked. He looked over the body of the chopper at her.

"No reason," she said. She didn't want to have to explain about her mother. Not now. "Hey, how did things go with Stan?"

"I gave him his job back," he said.

"Even though he stepped out on you and his wife?" she asked.

"He's a good business manager," he said. "He knows tax law, and besides, he's not the only one who stepped out."

"You mean…Irene?" Hailey gasped.

"With a pizza delivery guy. Stan walked in on them," he said.

"No!" Hailey gasped.

"'Fraid so," he said. "They do say there are always two sides."

"What's going to happen to them?" she asked.

"They're in counseling. They're going to try to fix

things. I gave Stan some more time off to regroup. He's going to need it."

Hailey couldn't believe it. Why... how was it that people always hurt the ones they were supposed to love the most? And she wondered if it would happen to her and Kid.

"Now what are you thinking about?" he asked.

"Nothing much," she said, not wanting to admit she was debating their future. "Okay, you naked."

"Whoa," he said with a grin. "Keep talking like that and I may have to close the shop early today."

Hailey felt herself grow hot. It was now or never. Why she was nervous she had no idea. Okay, yes, she did. She was afraid he would say no when she asked him to go to the auction with her, and she really wanted to go with him.

She wanted to walk in on his arm and spend the evening amongst her parents' peers with Kid. She wanted the rest of the world to see how wonderful he was and give her their blessing. Okay, so she was being delusional. Her mother would never bless the union of Billy "the Kid" Cassidy with her daughter, but maybe if the rest of her mother's circle accepted him... Hailey sighed. It was wishful thinking, indeed.

"Would you go with me to the auction?" she asked, not looking at him.

"What?" he asked.

"This chopper wouldn't exist without you," she said. "I'd really like for you to see how it does in the auction."

Kid was silent for a moment.

"Unless of course you have other plans."

"Actually, I've had my eye on this hot, young yoga instructor. If she didn't invite me, I was going to sit in my room and mope all night."

Hailey beamed at him. "You're going to look incredible in a tuxedo."

"Tuxedo?" he asked, looking horrified. "Can't I just wear one of those T-shirts that has a drawing of a tuxedo on it?"

"No," she said. "We can rent you one. And trust me, when you see the dress my mother picked out for me, you're going to want to blend in with the crowd."

"No need to rent," he said. "I own one. Since the brothers are all at varying stages of matrimony, we decided to chip in and buy matching tuxedos when my older brother was the first to take the dive. You'll love it. It's baby-blue polyester with a matching ruffled shirt."

"Then it will match the hideous dress that my mother picked out for me perfectly," Hailey laughed.

"Why did your mother choose your dress?"

"It's a long story," Hailey said. "But believe me when I tell you that it was a supreme act of sacrifice on my part."

"You'll be lovely in whatever you wear," he said, tucking a stray lock of hair behind her ear. Hailey felt breathless. The way Kid looked at her made her almost believe it.

"It's the formal equivalent of the orange suit I wore here the first day that I met you," she said. "My mother picked that one, too."

Kid cringed. "That was a bad one. It did have the redeeming quality of showing off your legs when you ran out of here."

"You noticed my legs?" she asked.

"Uh-huh," he said. "I'm definitely a leg man."

He leaned in close so that they were nose to nose. "Hailey Fitzwilly, you are a gem no matter what you are wearing, especially if it's just perfume."

Hailey leaned closer. "Is everyone gone?"

Kid looked over her shoulder at the garage. "Yup."

"Thank goodness," she said and launched herself into

his arms, sending him backward onto the concrete. Then she kissed him.

It didn't matter what anyone else thought about Kid Cassidy. The way he made Hailey feel about herself was the most amazing feeling she had ever had and she never wanted it to end.

WHEN HAILEY ARRIVED AT THE garage the next morning, Chooch didn't look happy. He was muttering and cursing and slamming tools, very uncharacteristic for the generally jovial Chooch.

"Is there something I can help with?" she asked.

"Not unless you can get the wiring right on that," he said and pointed to her chopper.

"What?" she asked. A sick feeling of dread crept across her skin.

Hailey hurried into Kid's office. He was just hanging up the phone.

"What's going on?" she asked, trying not to sound as if she was panicking.

"Chooch is having his usual finishing-the-chopper meltdown," Kid said and shrugged. "Don't worry."

"But the auction is tomorrow night and there is going to be TV coverage of you."

"Of me? Peaches, what have you done now?" he asked.

"It's just a short blurb about you and the chopper on the local news. It'll be painless. I promise."

Kid sighed.

"But that chopper has to work. It's the whole story. And look at it. It's beautiful," she said.

"Don't worry," Kid said. "It'll be working. I promise."

Hailey looked at him.

"Don't worry," he repeated.

Hailey took a deep breath. "How can I help?"

"Go get us some of Hank's superstrength coffee," he said. "We're going to need it."

She frowned.

"I'm kidding," he said.

Hailey looked over her shoulder at him as she walked toward Hank's.

"What are you going to do if we can't get it working?" Chooch asked as she walked away.

"We'll get it working," Kid said. "I promised we would and we will."

AT SUNSET, THE CHOPPER STILL wouldn't start. Kid and Chooch ordered a pizza and prepared to stay as late as possible to get the chopper running. Kid sent Hailey to teach her classes and told her he'd meet her at her place later.

At nine o'clock, Hailey was alone in her apartment sitting in front of her fish tank, wondering if she should call Kid or leave him alone. If it wasn't going well, she didn't want to bother him. But maybe he could use the moral support. Hailey waffled. This was the problem with new relationships—you didn't know the other person well enough to make these decisions and you generally had to learn by guessing wrong.

Hailey watched her fish. Two of the mollies were swimming around the faux castle that sat in the bottom of their tank. They looked happy together. *Okay,* she thought, *if they keep swimming together around the castle, I'll call him and if they separate around the castle, I won't call.* The two fish disappeared into the castle.

"Hey, that wasn't an option," she said and frowned. Even her fish were no help. "I'll give it one more hour. Then I'll call."

But after two pints of ice cream and three glasses of

wine, Hailey was fast asleep, facedown on her futon. This was where Kid found her in the wee hours of the morning.

Her brown hair was tumbled across her face. She had a smear of chocolate ice cream over her lip. Kid rolled her gently into his arms. She grunted as he carried her down the hall to her bedroom.

"What time is it?" she asked in voice throaty with sleep.

"One-thirty," he said.

"Did you get it fixed?" she asked.

"No." He tried not to sound grim, but he must have failed because her eyes popped open and she gave him a look fraught with worry. "I have a guy coming in tomorrow. I think he'll be able to figure it out."

"But it has to be finished by—" she began, but Kid put a hand over her mouth.

"Tomorrow night. I know," he said. "Don't worry. We'll get it done. I promise."

Hailey settled back into his arms with a sigh of relief. Kid envied her confidence in him. He hoped like hell they'd get it figured out tomorrow. The thought of disappointing Hailey was disturbing.

He wasn't sure when it had happened. Maybe it was that first fated day when she'd shown up in that butt-ugly suit. Or maybe it was the first time her hair had fallen down her back in a tumble of curls. It didn't really matter. The damage was done. He was in love with her. For good, bad or worse, she had managed to capture his heart.

Kid watched her while she slept. She was lovely, with her butter-soft skin and equally scrumptious curves. A small smile played on her lips and he wondered what she was dreaming about.

He'd been surprised when she'd asked him to go to the auction with her. She hadn't needed to do that. He'd been

sent a bunch of complimentary tickets that he had un-
loaded on his staff and business associates. He wondered
if she'd done it because of the chopper or because she'd
come to care for him, too.

He'd like to pretend the answer didn't matter to him,
but that would be a lie. He wanted Hailey to be proud to
be seen with him and he wanted her to be with him because she loved him. Well, one thing was certain—he'd
know tomorrow night. If she ditched him for Beemer Boy
and left him talking to the floral arrangements then he'd
know that was as far as they were going. But maybe she'd
surprise him and make their relationship public.

A cautious hope lifted his spirits. He was more nervous
about this public outing with Hailey than he was about
whether the chopper would be working or not. Choppers
he understood, but women…forget about it.

Kid pulled Hailey close and wrapped himself about
her, letting sleep claim him at last.

HAILEY WALKED INTO THE GARAGE to a string of curses that
would have caused her mother to faint. This was not a good
sign. Kid, Chooch, Uncle Pete, Mikey and another man
Hailey didn't recognize were all hovered over the yellow
chopper. It was in pieces. Hailey stifled a gasp. Her baby!

"What's happening?" she asked, rushing forward.

Kid's head snapped up. His face looked grim. He had
left before dawn, not even rousing her to say goodbye.

"It's bad, isn't it?" she asked. "You can tell me. I can
take it."

"It won't start," he said.

"We're going to have to scrap the whole electrical system," the newcomer said. Judging by his weathered skin,
he was just a few years younger than Uncle Pete. He wore
his gray hair in a ponytail that reached halfway down his

back. His grease-stained T-shirt made a valiant effort to hold in his potbelly but failed. In contrast to his belly, the seat of his jeans sagged. As if years of riding a motorcycle had caused his rear end to disappear or become concave. One of his front teeth was gold, and it flashed at Hailey when he delivered the bad news.

"Hi, I'm Hailey," she said and extended her hand.

"Paulie," he said in a gruff New York accent and grasped her hand in his meaty one.

"So, what are we going to do?" she asked.

"Scrap the electrical," Kid said.

"Can we do that? Do we have time?" she asked.

"We'll take it to Paulie's," Kid said.

"What can I do?" she asked.

"Start polishing," Kid said. "When we get the new system, we'll have no time to lose to put it all together," he said. "You ready, Paulie?"

"Let's ride," the older man said.

Hailey watched as they hurried to the van and left. Her stomach clenched, but she forced herself to breathe. Kid would pull this off. She knew he would.

The clock moved forward as if it belonged in a different time zone. They were never going to make it. Afraid to leave the garage in case Kid showed up, Hailey called Madeline and asked her to deliver her dress to the garage. She was going to have to dress here if they were going to make it on time.

In the meantime, she polished every part of the chopper possible and then she began to clean in earnest. Chooch and Uncle Pete leaped out of the way when they saw her coming at them with the shop vacuum. Mikey hid in the bathroom when she began to scour the grout on the tile floor in the kitchenette. She was just rinsing the floor when Madeline arrived with Charlotte in tow.

"Hailey, you're cleaning," Madeline said suspiciously. "What's wrong?"

"The chopper doesn't work," Hailey said. "It's due to be at the auction in less than six hours and it doesn't work. Kid is out trying to get a new electrical system for it. I think I'm having a nervous breakdown."

"Looks like we got here just in time," Charlotte said. "Let's go see if we can fix your dress, because if you show up at the auction without the chopper and in that dress, they'll stone you to death for sure."

"I can't leave," Hailey said. "If Kid shows up, I have to be here."

"Do you trust me to alter it for you?" Charlotte asked.

"I don't think you could possibly make it any worse," Hailey said. "Have at it."

Charlotte jumped up with excitement. "I know you think it is hideous, but it can be made beautiful. I'll have it back to you by five."

The sound of a sliding door opening on a van interrupted whatever Hailey would have said. "Kid's back! Okay, I'll meet you here at five."

Madeline and Charlotte dashed out of the garage while Hailey raced out to meet Kid.

"Did you get a new electrical system?" she asked.

"Yeah," he said and glanced at his watch. "Let's do it."

Together they worked on the chopper. The new system passed all of its bulb tests and it looked good. Hailey polished the chrome again as they went. It took two solid hours with all five of them working on it, but finally the chopper was done.

Kid wheeled it out of the garage. They all stood staring at it. The yellow paint made the children's handprints pop out. All of the chrome sparkled. It was a beautiful sight in the late-day sun. Finally Kid handed Hailey the key.

"Give it a try," he said.

Hailey felt her palms get sweaty and she wiped them against her coveralls.

She turned the key and hit the start button. It clicked and then the engine roared. Kid reached over and turned the throttle and the engine revved. It worked! Its mechanical purr was the greatest sound Hailey had ever heard, and she jumped into Kid's arms and peppered him with kisses. The men behind them exchanged proud high fives. They had done it.

"Hop on," Kid said and Hailey scrambled onto the back of the chopper. Together they took it around the block for a test drive.

Hailey wrapped her arms tightly about Kid's chest. It was hard to believe that one month ago she had taken a very different ride with him. It was hard to believe that their project was over now. She would no longer report to the garage for work. She clutched Kid more tightly. What would become of them now? She didn't know. And she realized she didn't like the fact that she didn't know.

Kid drove back to the garage and parked amidst the waiting crowd. Hailey slid off and moved to stand beside Charlotte and Madeline, who had just arrived. They were beaming, and she knew it wasn't because they were happy about the chopper. Apparently the dress alteration had been a success.

Kid switched off the engine and turned to Mikey.

"Let's load it up in the van," he said. "If we're going to get it there in time, we have to leave right now."

"But I want to go with you," Hailey said.

"Oh, no," Charlotte said. "You need hair and makeup—and fast. Kid, we'll bring her back in two hours. Be ready."

"Yes, ma'am," he said with a mock salute.

Madeline and Charlotte led Hailey across the parking lot, but Hailey turned back and said, "Be careful with her."

Kid smiled and nodded.

Four more steps and Hailey spun around and shouted, "Don't let anyone touch her. No fingerprints on her chrome."

Kid nodded and chuckled.

Just before she turned around the corner of Hank's Diner, she grabbed the wall to stop Madeline and Charlotte from dragging her off and shouted, "Make sure she's wrapped up so she doesn't get banged up on the drive."

Kid burst out laughing.

"I think we've converted her," Uncle Pete said. "Gosh, it's going to break her heart when someone wins this chopper."

"Maybe," Kid said.

HAILEY COULD BARELY SIT STILL in the hairdresser's chair. She wanted to know if the chopper got to the auction all right. She wanted to see it and make sure that none of its paint was scratched. She had never really understood the attraction of the chopper, but this was more than that because she had built this with Kid. It was her—no, *their*—baby.

Annoyed with Hailey's wiggling, the hairdresser heaved a huge sigh and abandoned the elaborate coiffure she'd been attempting. Instead, she let Hailey's hair go in a mass of bouncing curls. It flattered her heart-shaped face, making her appear delicate—not an adjective Hailey would ever use to describe herself. Next the cosmetologist took over. One stabbing in the eye with the eyeliner cured Hailey's wiggling for the rest of the session.

"You look like a model," Madeline muttered, making Hailey blush.

They raced back to Charlotte's shop with a half hour to spare.

"Your gown is in the fitting room," Charlotte said. "Holler if you need help with it. Nice hair, by the way."

"Thanks," Hailey said. She ducked behind a curtain. Her dress was hanging on a hook and Hailey squinted at it. Surely this couldn't be the same dress. Her mouth formed a tiny O as she gently took it off the hanger.

This was not the dress her mother had picked out. Oh, the feathers were still there, but they were nicely confined to the skirt. The top was now a sheer, formfitting, shell-pink bodice that hugged Hailey in all the right places and wrapped seductively around her shoulders, making her look busty and feminine and demure all at the same time. The feathered skirt made her look sultry and glamorous as the white feathers rippled over the darker pink fabric beneath them. The dress was flirty and outrageous but beautiful. Hailey felt her eyes well up with tears.

"Hailey, are you all right?" Charlotte asked, her voice impatient with obvious excitement.

"I'm fine. In fact, I'm freaking gorgeous," Hailey said as she threw back the curtain and stepped out of the tiny dressing room.

Madeline gasped and Charlotte chortled with triumph. She danced around Hailey, eyeing her from every angle.

"You are my finest creation," she said.

"How did you come up with this?" Hailey asked.

"Bottom of one dress with the top of another," Charlotte said. "I stole the idea from Oscar de la Renta. Not too shabby. If anyone asks where you got your dress, refer them to me. I think I am going to start designing."

"You are going to be the hottest thing since spandex," Madeline said. "Hailey, if Kid isn't in love with you already, this will do him in."

"Oh, I don't know," Hailey said. "I'm not really sure what we are. I'm not even sure if we'll be anything after tonight."

"Please," Charlotte said. "I've seen the way he looks at you. You're something all right. You're the girl who landed her Prince Charming. And to clinch it, I tossed out those ugly shoes you were going to wear and found you some Manolos that are positively Cinderella. They're pale pink with a delicate silver swirl on top and an edgy lucite heel. Perfect."

"I can't afford Manolos," Hailey gasped, even as her hands reached for the shoes.

"Don't worry." Charlotte laughed. "They're just loaners from my own closet. I want them back tomorrow or I turn you into a pumpkin."

"You have my word," Hailey said as she slid them onto her feet. They were fabulous.

"And now the final piece," Madeline said. "A vintage clutch purse in silver satin."

"Oh, it's darling," Hailey said. "How can I ever thank you two? Not to beat the Cinderella theme to death, but I swear you two are my fairy godmothers."

"Nah." Charlotte waved her hand. "We're just doing our civic duty not to let one of our own go out and make an ass of herself."

"Well, I can't thank you enough."

"Just have a ball tonight and give us all of the dirt tomorrow," Madeline said. "You have three minutes to get back to Kid's garage if you're going to leave for the auction on time."

Hailey kissed them each on the cheek and darted for the door. The Chop Shop was just around the block and there was no need to run, but she couldn't resist kicking up her heels a bit and enjoying the delightful sensation of feathers floating around her. She felt as if she were flying.

She passed a coffee shop and felt the admiring glances of several men and the speculative glances of several women. It was intoxicating. She rounded the corner, and in the light of the old street lamp, she saw him. She stumbled to a halt. He was gorgeous in a black Armani tuxedo that molded to his shoulders, making him look long and lean and incredibly Cary Grant suave. He took a step towards her and then paused.

"Peaches?" he asked as if he couldn't believe it was her.

"Hi," she whispered, feeling suddenly silly and self-conscious in the feathered dress. "Charlotte fixed my dress. Actually she cut it in half. But I think it's very nice."

Kid silently walked towards her. A foot away from her, he cupped her chin and tipped her face toward his. His eyes were full of wonder and he said, "Nice doesn't cut it, Peaches. You are breathtaking."

Then he kissed her. It was a long, slow, sweet kiss that melted Hailey all the way down to her borrowed shoes. Suddenly the auction didn't seem so important. At least, no where near as important as standing here kissing this man.

Kid pulled back and sucked in a gulp of air. "I am going to have to keep my distance or we aren't going to make it to the auction."

He tucked her hand around his elbow and walked her toward a car parked at the curb in front of his garage. It was a lovely blue Jaguar.

Hailey looked at him in surprise.

"What?" he asked with a smile. "You didn't think I was going to make you ride my Harley, did you?"

"I hadn't really thought about it."

"Some people collect stamps," he said. "I collect vehicles. It's a problem."

"How many do you have?" she asked as he handed her into the car.

"Fifteen," he said.

Hailey waited until he got in on the other side.

"Fifteen?" she repeated. "Where do you keep them all?"

"I loan them out to my brothers or friends," he said. "I'm working on it. I'm sure there must be a twelve-step program for this. I'm just not ready to get help yet."

"Maybe you could collect something else," she said.

"Such as?"

"Troll dolls?" she offered.

"No," he laughed.

"Beer-bottle caps?"

"No."

"Thimbles? That'd be a nice, manly display at the garage," she said.

He snorted.

"I enjoy you," he said and planted a kiss on her.

It made Hailey dizzy.

They drove silently toward the auction at the Claremont Hotel. Hailey couldn't believe the magic between them. They were a perfect fit. She loved him. It hit her fiercely and all-consumingly. She loved this man. She wanted to be with him and spend her life with him and have a family with him. Wow.

If her mother didn't have a stroke at the sight of her altered dress, Hailey was sure she'd faint dead away when Hailey very publicly announced to the auction attendees that Kid Cassidy was her boyfriend. Her stomach knotted and Hailey gulped. She could do this. She knew she could.

THE CLAREMONT HOTEL, WHICH was adjacent to the Fairfield County Children's Hospital, had hosted the auction in its grand ballroom every year since its inception. When Kid turned into the hotel's parking lot and handed his keys to the valet, Hailey glanced over at the hospital.

She didn't want to forget what this auction was all

about. It wasn't about dressing like a princess and feeling like one; it was about helping the children.

As Kid helped her out of the car, she smiled up at him and said, "Do you want to go visit some friends before we go to the auction?"

He followed the direction of her gaze and said, "Yes, but don't you think they deserve to see the finished product? I did promise them, after all."

"What do you mean?" she asked.

"Let's show them the chopper," he said. "Come on."

They hurried into the hotel. The auction hadn't officially begun yet and wouldn't for another hour.

The chopper was parked in the exhibits wing with a bunch of other big-ticket items. It gleamed in the light and Hailey felt her chest expand with pride.

Kid undid the safety lock and wheeled the chopper toward a rear exit.

"Excuse me!" a voice shouted. "Where are you going with that? It belongs to the auction."

Hailey spun around and saw one of the committee ladies bearing down on them in a purple ball gown that made her look like a giant eggplant with attitude.

"It's all right, Millicent," Hailey said with a smile and a wave. "It has…uh…a spark plug that won't spark. Mr. Cassidy is just taking it outside for a quick repair."

Millicent Meadows squinted at her. "Hailey Fitzwilly, is that you? Why, I didn't recognize you, dear. Interesting gown."

They air-kissed each other's cheeks.

"Thank you. I was going for 'interesting,'" Hailey said. "You look as pretty as always. I'll just go keep Mr. Cassidy company while he does his repair. Back in a flash."

"See that you are," Millicent said sharply. "The auction starts in fifty minutes."

Once outside, Kid grinned at her. "The spark plug won't spark? Clever."

"Thank you. I try." She shrugged.

"Well, hop on," Kid said. "You're going to have to side-saddle it. That okay?"

"No problem," Hailey said as she gently squashed her feathers onto the back of the seat.

With a roar of the engine, they zipped over to the Children's Hospital. Kid drove the chopper right into the main doors, cutting the engine in the lobby. As if they'd been expecting them, a gaggle of kids greeted them.

Nurse Sophie was there and so were Matty, Jamie, Luke and Sarah, along with a bunch of children Kid had yet to meet. They had been looking out the lobby window toward the hotel.

"You brought it to show us?" Matty exclaimed.

"I promised, didn't I?" Kid asked as he and Hailey scooted off the bike so that the kids could admire it.

Kid picked up Matty and Jamie and let them sit astride it. Matty beamed and made loud revving noises as he grabbed the handlebars and pretended to steer.

"Hey, this is my handprint," Sarah exclaimed from the back fender.

The kids swarmed the chopper, all searching for their handprints. Hailey exchanged a look with Kid. This made it all worthwhile. He winked at her and she could tell he felt the same way.

"Ah!" A gasp caused Hailey to turn. There stood little Brianna in her Little Mermaid pajamas. Her hands were clasped to her cheeks and her eyes were wide with wonder.

"You are a princess," she breathed. Her fingers reached out and gently stroked the velvety softness of Hailey's feathered dress.

"Thank you, Brianna," Hailey said and scooped the girl

into a hug. "That's the nicest thing anyone has ever said to me. Tell you what. When I am done with it, you can have it for the dress-up chest in the playroom, okay?"

"Really?" Brianna stroked the feathers and sighed.

"Children, it is past lights-out time," Nurse Sophie said. "And our prince and princess need to get to the ball."

Matty and Jamie slid off the chopper and stood nearby while Hailey and Kid climbed back on. When Kid revved the engine, the kids jumped and then giggled. A chorus of goodbyes sent them on their way.

The moon shone brightly in the dark sky, and for a fleeting moment, Hailey wished that she and Kid could just ride forever. In seconds they were back at the rear door to the hotel. Hailey hopped off the chopper and opened the door so that Kid could wheel it into place.

Millicent was standing there with her foot tapping.

"Everything is working, I trust?"

"Purring like a cat," Kid said as he returned it to its spot. "Would you care for a drink, Hailey?"

"Absolutely," she said and took his arm.

The guests for the auction were just beginning to trickle in. Hailey knew her mother liked to arrive fashionably late, so she figured she had about an hour before Selma made her appearance. Hailey decided to enjoy it. She would deal with her mother when the time came.

"Hailey, is that you?" A hand grabbed her elbow and gently spun her around away from Kid.

Hailey gasped. It was Burke.

10

"HAILEY, IT IS YOU," HE SAID. " I've been trying to catch up to you for days."

"Oh, hi, Burke," she said, feeling Kid's arm harden beneath her fingers. "I believe you've already met Kid Cassidy?"

Burke glanced over at Kid for the first time and straightened up. "At The Chop Shop, right? Pleasure to see you again."

"No, it's all mine," Kid said and he shook Burke's hand.

Hailey wondered if she was the only one to note the sarcasm in Kid's voice.

"Hailey, there is something very important that I need to speak with you about," Burke said.

"Now?" she asked.

"I'll go get our drinks," Kid said and stepped back.

"No," Hailey said. "Whatever Burke has to say to me, he can certainly say in front of you."

"I would prefer it to be just between us, Hailey." He looked earnest.

Hailey looked at Kid and nodded. She would give Burke his chance, but if he even hinted at them getting back together, she'd just have to shoot him down once and for all.

"I'll be right back," Kid said. He gave Burke a dark look and Hailey could tell he didn't like leaving them alone. To assuage his discomfort, she placed her hand on his forearm and before he could escape, she planted a kiss on his cheek.

"Hurry," she said.

"Yes, ma'am," he said with a warm smile.

Hailey watched him walk away and turned to find Burke watching her.

"Are you two a couple?" he asked, looking perplexed.

"Yes, we are," she said, tilting her chin defiantly. "Kid built the chopper that's in the silent auction tonight. He's a genius."

Burke raised his hands in surrender. "Does he make you happy?"

"Very," Hailey said.

"Then I think it's great," Burke said. "Hailey, I'm sorry I bailed out on you as abruptly as I did."

"You mean for being a sniveler and having your housekeeper dump me because my success bothered you?" she asked.

"Uh...yeah," he said, embarrassed. "I was a jerk."

"You'll get no argument from me, but it's all right," she said. "I'm doing great. I've never been happier."

"I can see that," he said. He gazed at her figure appreciatively and Hailey squirmed. What had she ever seen in him?

"I came here wanting to apologize and to tell you something."

"What was that?" she asked. She braced herself to let him down gently. Okay, not too gently.

"They've offered me the head of pediatrics position at the Children's Hospital."

"Oh," she said. This was not the declaration of undying love she'd been expecting to squash like a roach in her bathroom. "Well, that's terrific. You'll be fabulous."

She meant it. Burke may be a coward of a man, but he was a good doctor.

"Thank you." He looked down at his shoes. "I'm pleased. But I also wanted to tell you…"

"Oh, there you are." Selma Fitzwilly's voice cut off whatever Burke was about to say. "Look at you two. What a lovely couple. Dr. Burke, it is so good to see you again."

Selma engulfed Burke in a waft of perfume that was almost as strong as the grip she had on his arm. She was wearing a turquoise-blue beaded gown that jingled when she walked and must have weighed fifteen pounds. She turned to Hailey, and her brow lowered into a straight yet neatly waxed line above her eyes.

"What happened to your dress?" she asked.

"An unfortunate incident with my car. I was taking it out—very carefully—when it got caught on the door handle. Ripped it right in half." Hailey lied without blinking. She was really going to have to rekindle her relationship with the truth someday soon, but not right now. "A designer I know, Charlotte, fixed it. Isn't it lovely?"

Before Selma could answer, Burke said, "You're a vision, Hailey, as always."

Selma looked at him and closed her mouth. "Well, I won't keep you two. I'm sure you have important things to discuss. Hailey, your father went to bid on that monstrous chopper. I have to go make sure he doesn't win."

Hailey watched her walk away. Selma looked like a commander on a battlefield in her beaded gown. People parted for her as if they sensed she would go right over them like a Sherman tank if they didn't. One older gentleman in a leather vest and bolo tie actually leaped out of her way, dragging the two dowagers he had on his arms with him.

Hailey blinked. Leather vest? Bolo tie? It was Uncle Pete!

"Hailey, I have one other thing I need to tell you," Burke said.

"Uh, excuse me, Burke, it'll have to wait," Hailey said and she lifted her feathered skirt and hurried across the room toward Uncle Pete.

The crowd had filled the room to bursting, and she had to wangle her way through and around people, trying not to lose sight of Uncle Pete.

A waiter blocked her path and held out a tray of meatballs. Hailey grabbed two just to make him go away. She stuffed one in each cheek and hurried around the bar in the direction she'd seen Uncle Pete go.

Kid returned to the spot where he'd left Hailey only to find her and Burke gone. Damn. He'd gone to get drinks and been waylaid by a TV news crew. For that alone, he wanted to wring Hailey's neck. If she wanted this media stuff done right, she'd better not leave it up to him. He was pretty sure he hadn't used any profanity on camera, but it would have been nice to have her there.

Just where had she and Burke gone? He refused to panic. Just because they weren't where he'd left them didn't mean they had run off together. And why was he thinking that they would do that, anyway?

Because as he scanned the room, surrounded by Hailey's kind of people, he couldn't feel more out of place if he were buck naked and doing a two-step with a Viking hat on his head. He knew he was a good person and had no reason to feel inferior, but where he had calluses on his hands, they had manicures, even the men. It was disturbing.

He didn't see his lovely feathered girl in the crowd, so he decided to see if she'd gone to look at the chopper in the auction room. She was so proud of it. When she'd found a stray fingerprint on its chrome handlebars, she'd demanded his handkerchief so she could buff it out. She'd made quite the conversion over the past month, from a Vespa-riding granola eater to a granola-eating biker chick.

He had a vision of her in coveralls with a smear of grease on her cheek as she tried to convince the chopper that it would not beat her. That was his Hailey, the real Hailey. This society stuff was just fluff. He didn't have to worry, or so he kept telling himself.

An older woman swathed in a heavily beaded gown stood beside the chopper. She was shooing an older man away from the bidding clipboard. The man gave in with a laugh and a buzz on her cheek. She tried to look annoyed, but Kid saw the small smile that played on her lips. She looked oddly familiar, but he couldn't place her. This was not a woman with whom he had likely crossed paths.

He glanced at the bidding clipboard, which sat on a low table beside the chopper. *John Fitzwilly* was the last name scrawled. Ah! Hailey's father.

The woman looked from Kid to the chopper and back. Obviously she could tell he was not a regular attendee of such a social event.

"Are you Mr. Cassidy?" she asked.

"Yes, I am," he replied.

"I'm Selma Fitzwilly," she said and extended her hand. "Hailey's mother. I believe you know my daughter."

Kid shook her hand, stopping himself before he admitted how intimately he knew Hailey. "Yes, we've met."

"She speaks very highly of you," Selma said. "I didn't approve of a chopper as an auction item. They're too dangerous."

Kid said nothing.

"But I can't argue with the outrageous bids it has gotten," she said with a tsk.

Kid still said nothing. Hailey had not mentioned her parents much, and he wasn't sure they knew about her involvement with the garage or him. Besides, the more silent he was, the more Mrs. Fitzwilly would talk. Maybe he'd learn something about Hailey, or at the very least her family.

"Well, even though I don't approve, having garnered the highest-selling item ever will certainly stand Hailey in good stead with her future in-laws."

"I'm sorry, her future what?" Kid repeated. His voice was deceptively mild, as if he wasn't reeling inside.

"Well, it's not official," Selma said. "But I just left her talking with Dr. Burke, and I suspect he might be asking her right now. Won't that be wonderful? My Hailey married to a doctor—a pediatrician, no less. It's all I've ever wanted for her."

Kid looked at Selma as if she'd just kickboxed him in the groin. Selma was oblivious.

"Dr. Burke's parents are very prominent. She'll have membership to the best country club in the area. It's very exclusive. They won't even let me…well…never mind. That will change in short order, I can assure you."

"If you'll please excuse me," Kid said. "There's someone I must see."

"Oh, certainly. You've been a dear to listen to me prattle on. If you see my daughter and she isn't engaged—oh, dread the thought," Selma said, laughing at her own joke. "If she isn't occupied, please tell her I'd like to see her as soon as possible."

"Absolutely," Kid said and with a nod, he swept back into the main hall. He had to find Hailey before it was too late.

The noise of the crowd was so loud with chatter and laughter that Hailey could hardly hear herself think. The swing band had begun to play, making the room resonate with sound. Hailey gave up on trying to catch Uncle Pete and turned toward the French doors, hoping to get a breath of fresh air.

She hurried around the large ice sculpture of a swan that graced the center of the room, but then stopped short.

"Dad?" she spun to see her father laughing with a group of men adorned in tattoos and leather vests.

"Hailey, sweetheart," her father said and gave her a smacking kiss. He wobbled a little on his feet as he leaned forward.

"Dad, are you okay?" she asked.

"Never better," he said and snorted with laughter. "Justin here just made a drink luge out of this pretty little ice swan."

"A drink what?" she asked.

"Luge," Justin said and grinned at her. Pulling a Bic lighter out of his pocket, he held it to the back of the swan until the little trough was made a few drops deeper.

A lovely blonde wearing a red silk swatch of fabric over what were obviously store-bought bouncy D-cups held a bottle of tequila aloft.

"Who's next?" she asked.

Justin slapped Hailey's dad on the shoulder and said, "My man John is up for it, aren't you John?"

"Let her rip," John said and he placed his mouth on the swan's rump.

The blonde poured a shot of tequila that ran down the swan's back and into John's mouth. Hailey felt her jaw hit the floor. Her father was drinking tequila out of a swan's butt.

Everything started to go gray and she saw spots. Her dad was laughing, and one of his cronies came over and joined him. Hailey excused herself and slowly backed away. She needed air. She needed to put her head between her knees. She needed to run away.

"Hey, there, Peaches," Kid said as he grabbed her by the elbow and led her toward the edge of the crowd. "I've been looking all over for you."

"I need air," she said.

"Good, because I need to talk to you." They were half-way out the French doors when the band took a break and Caroline's voice boomed over the PA.

"Welcome to the fifteenth annual Fairfield County Children's Hospital charity auction." Caroline's silver sheath molded perfectly to her curves and showed off her black locks. "We are halfway through our event and there is only one more hour to bid on our silent-auction items. I'd like to take this time to thank Kid Cassidy of The Chop Shop for his incredibly generous donation of one of his world-renowned choppers."

A spotlight suddenly snapped on Kid and Hailey, trapping them in the room and blinding them as they waved to the wildly applauding crowd.

"I think I'm going to be sick," Hailey whispered to Kid. "It's too hot and too bright."

"Sneak out behind me," he said, giving her a gentle nudge. "I'll follow you as soon as they shut off that damned light."

Hailey didn't hesitate. She bolted through the doors and across the veranda, sucking in gulps of fresh air as she went.

The night was in shambles. What she had hoped would be one of the most romantic nights of her life was slowly turning into a drunken keg party at a frat house.

A large, warm hand rested on her back. "Hey, are you all right?"

Hailey turned to find Kid beside her. She leaned into his warm body and sighed. No matter what, she still had Kid.

"I really just needed air," she said. "I'm better now. I think the sight of my dad drinking out of a swan's behind was more disturbing than I was prepared for."

"I can see where it might be," Kid said.

Hailey couldn't resist him anymore. In a world gone crazy, here was Kid, rock solid and dependable. She yanked him close by his lapels and planted a kiss on him that should have ended their conversation…but it didn't.

He reluctantly pulled away from her and asked, "So what did the doctor want?"

"Who?" she asked.

"Burke," he said more emphatically.

"Oh, him. He got a job with the Children's Hospital," she said. "I guess he didn't want me to be caught by surprise."

"Is that it?"

"I guess so."

"Your mother seems to think he was going to propose," Kid said.

"My mother?" Hailey gulped. "You met my mother?"

"Why does she think Burke is going to propose?"

"Because she's delusional," Hailey said. "Actually it's not her fault. Burke and I dated for about six months almost a year ago. He had his housekeeper break up with me. The next thing I knew, he was living in Boston. My mother was so enamored with him, I never had the heart to tell her I'd been dumped. I thought if she didn't see him, in time she'd let it go…"

"He's a moron," Kid said. "Is he the reason you wanted me to come with you tonight?"

"What do you mean?"

"Were you trying to prove something to him?" he asked.

"No," she said. "I never cared enough about him to want to prove anything."

"Oh," Kid said, looking skeptical. "So you think your mother is way off base?"

"She's not even in the right stadium," Hailey said with

a shake of her head. "Now I have a question for you. I'm pretty sure I saw Uncle Pete schmoozing some crusty old debutantes. Did you give him and some of the other guys tickets?"

"You don't approve," he said as he took a step back from her.

"I didn't say that," she said. "I was just surprised."

"What's the matter? Are you afraid they don't fit in?" he asked.

"They don't," she said. "I saw Chooch spitting into a champagne flute. If my mother saw him, she'd drop on the spot."

"And heaven forbid we do anything to offend your mother," Kid said. "What's she going to say when she finds out you've been banging a mechanic?"

"Hey. Wait a minute," she said. "All I said was that I didn't know they'd be here. Why didn't you tell me?"

"Why does it matter?" he asked. "They helped build that chopper, so I gave them some tickets. They put in extra hours on other projects just so I could help you. They deserve to be here. They all contributed."

"No one said they didn't," Hailey said, feeling her temper heat.

"So what's your problem with them being here?" Kid asked.

"I never said I had a problem. I was just surprised," she said. "Jeez, what is bugging you?"

"Nothing," he said. "I guess I'd better go and corral the crew before they do anything to embarrass you."

Kid stalked back in the direction of the French doors. Hailey blinked after him. What the hell had just happened? One minute they'd been kissing and the next second he was as prickly as a week's worth of unshaven leg stubble.

Hailey rubbed her temples. What had she said? Had it

really been that offensive? She loved Uncle Pete and Chooch and all of the guys. But she had been surprised to see them here. She'd hoped to introduce Kid to her mother and show her that he could fit in just fine, but with the rest of the guys turning this into the social equivalent of a biker rally, Kid was not going to come off in a good light.

She'd expressed her surprise and Kid had taken it personally. How did he think she would react to having her worlds collide? Well, duh, she didn't like it. Who would? Especially when she had Selma to contend with.

A cool breeze sent her feathers ruffling and Hailey sighed. She'd had such different hopes for this evening. She'd wanted to have Kid by her side all night. To dance in his arms and drink champagne and let the whole world see how in love she was with him. Instead, she'd hardly seen him and now he was mad at her.

For a fleeting second, Hailey debated hopping onto her chopper and riding through the crowd until she found Kid. Then she'd force him on back and take off. The image made her smile even though she knew the stubborn mule of a man would probably refuse to get on, never mind the fact that she had yet to learn to drive the darn thing.

The French doors banged open and a wobbly couple stumbled out seeking privacy. Not wanting to be a voyeur, Hailey hurried past them and back into the auction. If nothing else, she should see that her father didn't spend any more time lugeing with the swan.

Hailey was halfway across the room when her mother intercepted her.

"Hailey, where have you been?" Selma asked. "I asked that nice Mr. Cassidy to tell you I was looking for you. Were you with Dr. Burke?"

"No, I…uh…nice Mr. Cassidy?" Hailey asked. "You like him?"

"He seems very nice, despite the facial hair and earrings," Selma said. "I heard Millicent Meadows tell her daughter that he's an up-and-comer. There's even a rumor that they want him to star in a reality show. Can you believe it? Maybe he'll get lucky and meet a nice young lady tonight."

Hailey closed one eye and studied her mother. She wondered if her mother was drunk. "You haven't been near the swan, have you?"

"No, why?" Selma asked.

"Have you seen Dad?" she asked.

"He's in the auction room again," Selma sighed. "I give up. He's a bidding fool tonight. So, tell me, what did Dr. Burke want? I don't see a ring on your finger."

Before Hailey could answer, the band stopped playing and Caroline Matthews took the stage again.

"Quiet, please, quiet," she instructed the crowd. The roar of conversation dimmed. "The auction has closed."

The crowd cheered.

"Before I announce the winners, I would like to introduce Dr. Gerard, the chief of staff of the Fairfield County Children's Hospital. He has a few announcements he'd like to share with us."

Dr. Gerard took the podium. He was a sweet man, but he was the world's slowest speaker. Hailey shifted from foot to foot. She scanned the crowd, looking for Kid. He was taller than most, but the lighting was dim. She couldn't see the outer reaches of the ballroom and wondered if maybe he was in the auction room.

"And so it is with great pleasure that I introduce to you our new head of pediatrics, Dr. Burke Masterson," Dr. Gerard said and the crowd erupted into applause.

"Oh, my!" Selma gripped Hailey's arm. "Did you know about this?"

"Yes, he told me," Hailey said, still looking for Kid.

Burke took the podium and gave a small smile.

"It's good to be home," he said. The crowd broke into more applause.

"I am honored to have been appointed to the position of chief of pediatrics, and I will do my best to make Fairfield County Children's Hospital the finest children's hospital in the country."

There was more applause, but Hailey wasn't listening. She saw Kid standing at the edge of the crowd. He was watching Burke as if trying to assess his worth. Hailey wondered why he cared. It wasn't as if she held any feeling greater than friendship for Burke. Then again, maybe he was wondering if Burke was a good choice for the children. Kid was the kind of person who would care that Burke was good with kids, not just that he came from a good family.

"They say that every good man has a better woman at his back," Burke continued. Selma's fingers squeezed into Hailey's forearm like talons.

"Ouch!" Hailey grabbed her mother's fingers in hers before she drew blood.

"Do you hear that?" Selma hissed. "He's going to mention you."

"I am lucky enough to have such a woman."

Hailey could feel Kid's gaze upon her. She refused to meet his stare, uncertain of what she would see there and not feeling brave enough to look.

"If you will indulge me, I would like to take a moment in this very public place to ask this very special woman if she will do me the honor of becoming…"

"We accept!" Selma shrieked. She jumped up and down in her fifteen-pound gown and clapped her hands as tears poured from her eyes.

Hailey looked at her mother and then at Burke. She felt

as if she were watching a car crash. Everything seemed to be moving in slow motion, but before she could stop it, she was standing on stage next to Burke with her mother sobbing beside her.

Hailey looked into the crowd to find Kid, but only saw her father waving drunkenly at her as he tipped his glass and said, "Welcome to the family…." He paused and then burped.

A door closed at the back of the hall and Hailey knew that it was Kid leaving her.

She turned to Burke and they spoke at once. "I can't marry you."

"What?" they each asked.

"*What?*" Selma shrieked.

"I'm sorry, Hailey, I wasn't proposing to you," Burke said. "I was proposing to her. That's the other thing I wanted to tell you. I love her."

He pointed to a lovely blonde in an ice-blue gown standing off to the side. She looked completely unruffled by the past few minutes, unlike Hailey, who didn't know whether to throw up or pass out. The blonde was perfect for Burke.

Hailey started to laugh.

"I'm so relieved," she said. "I'm in love with Kid. I want to marry him."

"Ahhh." Selma went down in a puddle of turquoise beads. Burke had the good grace to catch her before she hit the floor.

"I have to go and find him," she said to Burke over her mother's supine form.

"But what about your mother?" he asked.

"You're a doctor," Hailey said. "She couldn't be in better hands. Besides, you owe me one for having your housekeeper dump me."

She hurried off the stage, pausing by the blonde to say, "I hope you two will be very happy together."

The blonde smiled and said, "Same to you."

Hailey rushed out of the auction hall and into the dark night. She looked both ways up and down the street. Kid's Jaguar was still in the valet parking, but there was no sign of him.

"He's gone," Chooch said from where he was leaning on the side of the building.

"Where?" Hailey asked.

"Are you going to marry that doc?" Chooch asked.

"No, she isn't." Uncle Pete came out of the building with his pair of old ladies still circling his arms like a toddler's water wings. "If you'd stayed, you'd know she gave him the boot, just like I told Kid she would. I should have bet him more than a big-screen TV on that."

"You bet on that?" she asked.

"Yeah, but he didn't stick around to hear your answer," said Uncle Pete. "He just took the chopper and bailed."

"But someone won that chopper," Hailey said. "He can't just take it."

"That someone isn't going to know," Chooch said, but Uncle Pete gave him a harsh look.

"Of course they're going to know," Hailey said. "Of all the irresponsible, jackass maneuvers he could have pulled, that tops it. So, where did he go?"

"I don't know," Chooch shrugged.

"Baloney," Hailey said. "You two know him better than anyone. Where did he go?"

The two exchanged a look.

"It's hard to find," Chooch said. "It's a tiny shack down on a pier. They serve beer and seafood. They draw a pretty rough crowd on a Friday night."

"I don't care," Hailey said and wiggled her fingers at the valet. "Edward, give me the keys to the Jaguar."

The valet took them off of a hook and went to get the

car. Hailey stopped him with a hand on his arm. "Just give me the keys."

There must have been a maniacal look in her eyes that told him to drop the keys in her hand and back away, because that's exactly what he did.

Hailey stomped toward the Jaguar. She vaguely remembered the day just over a month ago when Kid had ordered her to climb onto his chopper. She had done it without question, just as she was going after him now.

The road was different at night. The orchard blossoms were gone as they began their metamorphosis into fruit. Sort of like her relationship with Kid. They'd started out as fragile as a blossom, but they were more substantial now. They were as strong as the apple trees that surrounded the road. Hailey knew it. She just had to convince Kid of the same.

She slowed the car at the end of the road. The chopper, her baby, sat parked all alone. Kid was here. She didn't know how to get to the pier directly, so she was going to have to hoof it up the beach and hope she could scale the wall in her silly dress.

She slipped off her pricey sandals and left them on the passenger seat. The sand was cold and damp between her toes. The bite of the salt air was refreshing. The soft sound of the small waves rolling up into the bay calmed her nerves, even though she had no idea what she was going to say to Kid.

What could she say to make him change his mind about her, about them?

She got to the stone wall that surrounded the pier and looked for a handhold or a foothold. She found none. Now what? She debated calling for help, but then Kid would hear her and probably bail again.

"Hey, lookee here," a voice shouted down at her. "I found me a mermaid. Give me your hand, honey, and I'll reel you in."

The man wobbled on his feet, and Hailey wondered if he'd wandered over here to pee. Great. Well, at least he still had his pants on.

Seeing no alternative, she took his hand. He hoisted her up the front of the rock and onto the pier.

"Have you seen Kid Cassidy?" she asked.

"Man, like he don't have all the luck," the man said, shaking his head with disgust. "Even the mermaids ask for him. Hey, aren't you supposed to grant me a wish?"

"A what?" she asked.

"A wish," he said. "I think that's the least you can do before I turn you over to Kid."

"What's your wish?" Hailey asked, looking over his shoulder.·

The pier was crowded with bikers. A few she recognized from the rally a few weeks ago, but there was no sign of Kid. He had to be here. The chopper was here.

"Well, now, I don't know." The drunk scratched his chin as he contemplated his wish.

"How about a cold beer?" Hailey asked.

"Just one?" the man asked.

"One for you and all of your friends," Hailey said. She reached into her clutch purse and pulled out a fifty. She smacked it into the man's palm and made her way around him toward the little restaurant.

"Hey, that's cold," the man grumped. "I think a guy should get a little nooky for saving a mermaid."

"A little what?" Hailey whirled around in outrage.

"A little nooky," he said. "I don't think that's asking much, is all."

"Are you crazy?" she snapped. "First, I am not a mermaid. Second, you didn't fish me out of the ocean. You helped me up a stone wall. Now go get drunk before I turn you into a toad."

"Yikes!" the man yelped and scurried around her toward the bar.

"Some people," Hailey said, glaring after him.

She made her way through the crowd. Silence greeted her as she moved between leather-clad men and women. It was a chilly night on the shore, but that didn't stop the women from wearing bikini tops and leather chaps over their thongs. Hailey felt about as welcome as a warden at a prison inspection.

"Hey, Kid, your date—or maybe she's your canary—is here," a woman with a throaty voice called and then she cackled with laughter. "I didn't know you were such a bird lover."

It was the buxom blonde Kid had been talking to at the biker rally. She looked as if she were hoping Hailey was about to crash and burn. Hailey put her chin up. Maybe she was, but she wasn't about to let this cow enjoy it.

The crowd parted and Hailey saw Kid leaning against the rail at the end of the pier. He was still in his tux, but his tie was undone and hung around his neck like a weary soldier. Hailey's heart gave a sharp pang when she saw him. What had he thought when he'd heard Burke begin to propose and her mother's ecstatic acceptance? It must have hurt badly. Had their positions been reversed, she was sure her heart would have felt as if someone had reached into her chest and pulled it clean out.

She wanted to throw herself into his arms, but good sense stopped her. Given her feathered outfit, she wasn't sure whether he'd send her for a swan dive off the pier and let her swim for it or not.

"You know, it's bad form to leave your date at the party without telling her that you're leaving," she said.

"True," he said. He looked at her then. His blue eyes revealed nothing and Hailey felt the breeze shiver across her shoulders. Maybe he didn't feel the same way about her and this was all just a huge mistake.

"But I think it's worse form, and you can check with Miss Manners on this, to accept a proposal from a man who is not your date."

"I think the key word there is *accept*," she said. "I didn't."

A small smile played at Kid's mouth. "Your mother did."

"She also fainted when Burke and I rejected each other," she said.

"Again, please," he said, peeling off his jacket and wrapping it about her shoulders.

"You heard right," Hailey said. "I said no, and Burke informed me that he wasn't proposing to me. He was proposing to a very beautiful blond woman who didn't bat an eye when my mother fainted right into his arms. She's perfect for him."

"You're not," Kid said as he drew her into his arms. "You like bad boys. Burke is not a bad boy."

"No, he isn't," Hailey said. "But you are and I love you."

"I love you, too, Hailey Fitzwilly," Kid said and then he kissed her.

A rowdy chorus of catcalls and suggestions to go get a room filled the night air, but Hailey and Kid were oblivious.

"You know, whoever won the chopper is going to be

miffed at you," Hailey said as she pulled away to take a breath.

"I think I can smooth it over," Kid said, still kissing her.

"How?" she asked.

"I'll just give her the keys," he said. Kid stepped back from her and reached into his pocket. He took her hand and turned it palm up, then he placed the key to the chopper, which was attached to a heart-shaped key chain, in her hand.

Hailey felt her throat tighten. "But how?" she asked.

"You worked so hard on it," he said. "I knew you'd be crushed if someone else won it. That's why all of the guys were there. I knew I couldn't bid on it, but they could. So I had them bid for me."

"Oh, Kid," Hailey sobbed and wrapped her arms about his neck. "I love you so much."

"And I love you," he whispered, his own voice thick with emotion. "Marry me?"

"Yes, yes, yes," she answered.

And then she kissed him. It was a soft, sweet kiss that swiftly turned electric.

"What are you thinking?" he asked as he pulled away and shook his head as if to clear it. Hailey liked that their kisses made him as dizzy as they made her. It was magic.

"That this would be a lovely spot for a wedding," she said.

"Won't your mother expect it to be at some ritzy country club?" he asked.

"I think it's time my mother got to know the real me," Hailey said. "Don't you?"

"Absolutely," Kid agreed. "I love the real you and I know your mother will, too."

"As long as I have you, it doesn't matter," Hailey said.

Kid held her close, and Hailey knew that it didn't matter what anyone else thought of them. Hailey knew she had found the perfect guy for her and that was all that mattered. She didn't need anyone's approval and didn't care if she disappointed anyone with her choice. She and Kid were going to live a long and happy life together, and she couldn't wait for it to start.

Epilogue

"ARE YOU SURE THIS IS THE PLACE, John?" Selma Fitzwilly asked her husband. "This can't be right."

"This is it," he said. "See? There's Jack."

Selma took her husband's arm as he led her down the wooden pier toward a group of tables covered in white linens with simple glass vases that held lovely bunches of delicate, peach-colored roses in them.

"They're getting married here?" Selma asked her son.

"Good to see you, too, Mom," he said and kissed her cheek. "No, actually they're getting married down there."

Jack pointed toward the small beach just past the pier. Folding chairs and a large arching trellis, decorated in more peach-colored roses, were set up just above the water's edge.

"We'll need to climb down the rocks to get to it," he said. "You might want to leave your shoes here."

"But these are Ferragamos," Selma protested. "And they match my dress."

She was wearing a tea-length navy gown with a flared skirt and a matching sheer navy shawl. It was very proper for a mother attending her daughter's wedding under protest.

"I'll carry you," John offered.

"Don't be ridiculous," Selma said. "You'll hurt your back, and you need to walk Hailey down whatever that is." She waved toward the beach in disgust.

"I'll carry you," Jack offered. "Want a piggyback ride, or would you rather jump and I'll catch you?"

"This is just so undignified," Selma said with a sniff. "Why couldn't she get married at the club?"

Just then two men arrived, wearing dress shirts with leather vests over them and jeans. More importantly, they were placing a short staircase from the pier to the beach below.

"Looks like your dignity has been saved," Jack said. He held out his arm and asked, "May I?"

"Oh, I suppose," Selma said and put her hand around Jack's elbow. Then she turned back to her husband and said, "Tell Hailey if she has a bout of bad stomach that I have some Pepto in my purse."

"I'll tell her," John said and gave her a kiss on the cheek.

The short walk across the beach was tricky, and sand poured into her Ferragamos, but Selma refused to let it show. She wouldn't allow anyone to see the hurt and humiliation she was suffering. Her pride wouldn't allow it.

It was bad enough that she'd had no say about the location of the wedding or the reception, but she hadn't been consulted on the invitations, the flowers or the guest list, either. Hailey had completely shut her out just because she said she didn't approve of Kid Cassidy. And really, as a good mother, why would she approve? He was a mechanic for pity's sake. What did he have to offer Hailey?

Yes, he was apparently an up-and-comer, but could he offer her social status? Could he offer her entry into the more prestigious bastions of society? No.

Selma leaned on Jack as they made their way through the chairs. A group of children sat toward the back, wiggling in anticipation. Selma tried to keep her eyes forward, but she couldn't help scanning the crowd. Men and women in a variety of leather ensembles filled many of the seats. His friends, no doubt.

Selma frowned and looked forward, but her eye was caught by Mr. and Mrs. Masterson—Burke's parents— and she gasped. What were they doing here? Beside them sat Burke with his bride-to-be. Selma pasted a smile on her face and was surprised to see Marcy Masterson smile at her in return.

"What are they doing here?" she whispered to her son Jack.

"They who?" he whispered back.

"The Mastersons," she hissed.

"Oh, Hailey and Burke's fiancée have really hit it off. She's interested in advertising and wants to open a small firm with Hailey. The four of them have been spending a lot of time together. And I hear that the Mastersons are so taken with Kid's generosity for the Children's Hospital that they are recommending him for membership in their club."

"No!" Selma said and stopped halfway down the aisle to stare at him.

"That's what I heard," he said.

Selma let Jack lead her to her seat. The folding chair was stiff and hard, but she hardly noticed. She glanced across the way and saw a small woman dressed in a lovely gown of yellow. The woman beamed at her and Selma found herself smiling back. The blue eyes were the same as Kid's. This had to be his mother. She looked kind. That was good. Hailey needed a kind mother-in-law.

Music began to play, a flute and an oboe off to the side of the trellis, and Jack came to sit beside her. A minister wearing simple vestments led Kid Cassidy and an older gentleman down the far side of the chairs to stand in front of the altar.

Kid looked very handsome in his black tuxedo, and Selma could see why Hailey had been taken with him. He winked at his mother and she shook her head and smiled at him. He certainly had a rogue's charm. Then he looked at Selma. He smiled at her with an understanding that almost made her weep, then he winked at her and Selma felt her face grow warm. A rogue indeed.

The music grew louder and everyone's attention was drawn back to the pier. A boy of about eight wearing a black suit and a young girl in a lovely white dress stood at the top of the stairs. Together they made their way down the stairs. The girl tossed peach-colored petals on the ground while the boy clutched a delicate ring-bearer's pillow in his hands. When they reached the sand, the boy wobbled a bit but righted himself. As they made their way through the chairs, the boy's limp was hardly discernable, but Selma saw it and knew he was one of the children from the hospital. His face was set with determination while the girl at his side beamed at everyone and tossed her petals as if she were a fairy in a fairy tale. When they reached the makeshift altar, the girl went to stand on the bride's side and the boy went to stand beside Kid. Kid stopped him and whispered something in his ear. The boy grinned and it was as if someone had turned on a light.

Kid's words had gone unheard by most of the crowd, but Selma had heard him. He'd told the boy he was proud of him. Selma felt her heart pinch. Kid was a good man.

A lovely woman with long, black hair, wearing a simple dress of powder-blue with embroidered flowers of the same color along the hem and halter neckline, came next. As she came closer, Selma recognized her as the woman Hailey ran a yoga studio with. Meredith...no...Madeline was her name.

That had been another shock. In the days following the

auction, Hailey had informed them that she was marrying Kid and, oh, by the way, she owned a yoga studio. Selma was still trying to swallow that one. She felt Jack straighten up in his seat as Madeline walked by. She looked at his face. He looked besotted.

The music swelled again and the crowd rose to its feet. Hailey appeared at the top of the stairs. Selma felt her breath catch in her throat. Her baby girl was breathtaking. John whispered something in her ear and Hailey laughed. Together they made their way down the stairs, across the sand and down the aisle. As Hailey drew closer, Selma felt the tears in her eyes well up again, because Hailey was wearing Selma's old wedding dress.

Jack handed her his handkerchief and Selma dabbed her eyes. The dress had been restyled to fit Hailey, but Selma would have known it anywhere. A white organza overskirt embroidered with white daisies and boasting a simple halter neckline—it had been chic in 1972, and now her baby girl was wearing it and it was just beautiful.

She glanced at her husband, resplendent in his tuxedo with their daughter on his arm. She had no doubt as to how Hailey had gotten her dress, and she couldn't have been more grateful. It occurred to her then that everything she had ever wanted for Hailey was coming true. As she watched the looks exchanged between Hailey and Kid, she could see the love flow between them. Hailey was marrying a man as wonderful as Selma had found for herself thirty-three years before. What more could Selma want for her? Nothing.

John stood beside Hailey until the minister asked, "Who gives this woman to this man?"

Selma rose from her seat and moved to stand beside John. He smiled at her, and together they said, "We do."

Hailey turned and sighed, "Oh, Mom."

Selma hugged her close and said with a tight voice, "Don't cry, dear, you'll ruin your face. Just be happy, honey, and know that I love you and I always will."

"I love you, too, Mom."

John kissed Hailey's cheek and placed her hand in Kid's. As Hailey turned to face Kid, Selma settled back into her seat. They were going to have beautiful children. She would have to be on hand to make sure her grandbabies got into the right schools and the right activities. There would be no motorcycles for any of her grandsons. As Hailey and Kid sealed their vows with a kiss, Selma sighed with contentment. Everything was going to be just fine.

Seduction and Passion Guaranteed!

They're the men who have everything—
except brides…

Wealth, power, charm—what else could a
heart-stoppingly handsome tycoon need?
In the GREEK TYCOONS miniseries you have
already been introduced to some gorgeous Greek
multimillionaires who are in need of wives.

**Now it's the turn of favorite Presents
author Lucy Monroe,
with her attention-grabbing romance**

THE GREEK'S INNOCENT VIRGIN
Coming in May
#2464

Are you getting it at least twice a month?

Here's how: Try RED DRESS INK books
on for size & receive two FREE gifts!

Bombshell
by Lynda Curnyn

As Seen on TV
by Sarah Mlynowski

YES! Send my two FREE books.
There's no risk and no purchase required—ever!

Please send me my two FREE tradesize paperback books and bill me just 99¢ for shipping and handling. I may keep the books and return the shipping statement marked "cancel." If I do not cancel, about a month later I will receive 2 additional books at the low price of just $11.00 each in the U.S. or $13.56 each in Canada, a savings of over 15% off the cover price (plus 50¢ shipping and handling per book*). I understand that accepting the two free books places me under no obligation ever to buy any books. I can always return a shipment and cancel at any time. Even if I never buy another book from Red Dress Ink, the free books are mine to keep forever.

160 HDN D367   360 HDN D37K

Name (PLEASE PRINT)

Address   Apt. #

City   State/Prov.   Zip/Postal Code

*Want to try another series? Call 1-800-873-8635
or order online at www.TryRDI.com/free.*

In the U.S. mail to: 3010 Walden Ave., P.O. Box 1867, Buffalo, NY 14240-1867
In Canada mail to: P.O. Box 609, Fort Erie, ON L2A 5X3

*Terms and prices subject to change without notice. Sales tax applicable in N.Y.
**Canadian residents will be charged applicable provincial taxes and GST.
All orders subject to approval. Offer limited to one per household.
® and ™ are trademarks owned and used by the trademark owner and/or its licensee.

© 2004 Harlequin Enterprises Ltd.

RED DRESS INK

RDI04MMP

HARLEQUIN®
flipside

Be sure to catch your favorite
Harlequin Flipside authors
writing for other Silhouette
and Harlequin series!

SILHOUETTE *Romance*®

Holly Jacobs
in Silhouette Romance

ONCE UPON A PRINCESS
May 2005

ONCE UPON A PRINCE
July 2005

ONCE UPON A KING
September 2005

Also watch for:

Stephanie Doyle in Silhouette Bombshell in July 2005

Elizabeth Bevarly, Cindi Myers and Dawn Atkins
appearing in Harlequin Blaze in Fall 2005

Stephanie Rowe writing for Harlequin Intrigue in 2006

Barbara Dunlop in Silhouette Desire in 2006

Look for books by these authors at your favorite retail outlet.

www.eHarlequin.com   HFAIOS